JAYLA JUMPS IN

JAYLA JUMPS IN

JOY JONES

ALBERT WHITMAN & COMPANY
CHICAGO, ILLINOIS

Thanks to the Wednesday Night Writing Group,
DC Retro Jumpers, and Sara Camilli.

CHAPTER 1

I knew where babies came from, and I wanted one. Time was running out. Pretty soon I'd be too old to have any fun with another kid in the family. I was already eleven years old, and I still didn't have a baby brother or sister. My parents needed to get busy. Maybe today would be the day I'd ask them for a sibling.

Today was Thanksgiving—one of my least favorite holidays. Why? Well, it's the only holiday that comes with homework. Nobody makes you write a book report about Christmas or take a test about Valentine's Day. You don't get any presents. If you're the only kid in your family, you're stuck listening to a bunch of boring grown-ups talk. And if there are other kids in your family, well, hopefully they're better than my cousins.

We always celebrated Thanksgiving with my mother's side of the family, and the kids on that side could be pretty horriful. Antwon was my age—eleven—and he was about as sharp as an eraser. Earlier that afternoon, he had come into the kitchen and said to my mom, "Can I help out, Aunt Sherry?" To offer to do any work, he must have been bored to death, too. Anyway, my mother gave him the big blue box of salt and told him to fill the saltshaker. He was sitting at the dining room table hunched over and leaning in the way kids do when they have a complicated word problem to solve. I went over to see what had him concentrating so hard. He was actually trying to drop each grain of salt one-by-one through those tiny holes.

"Antwon, there's an easier way to do that," I said, coming to his side.

"Really? It's hard putting each drop into these skinny holes!"

"I'll help you. Do this." I unscrewed the top of the saltshaker, then opened the spout on the box of salt. As I positioned his hands so that he could pour the salt into the shaker, he looked at the process as if we were doing a magic trick.

"Wow, Jayla, you're real smart!" And then he gave me a big, warm smile.

It made me feel a little bit ashamed for calling him dumb, even if it was only inside my head.

They call Uncle Jimmy's boys Tommy and Kwame the Human Tsunami. Uncle Jimmy only gets them for the long Thanksgiving weekend, then he doesn't have them again till school lets out at Christmas. He and his kids' mom broke up, so he isn't around them that much and doesn't know how to make them behave. They break everything they touch. I avoided them, although sometimes they could be funny to watch as long as you stayed far enough away that you didn't get in trouble along with them.

I also stayed away from Shontessa. She was your typical stuck-up teenage snob. Every year she would brag that she was going to be getting the coolest sneakers or latest iPhone or some other blingy thing come Christmas. She claimed she had one thousand followers on Instagram. She said she met the real Hello Kitty at the mall. She told me she had gone to a Drake concert and he kissed her backstage. Shontessa was such a huge boaster and bragger. I wouldn't believe anything she said even if she swore she was lying.

Most of the family was sitting around the living room, waiting for the food to be ready. It was Daddy's idea that we should each say what we're grateful for. Aunt Juicy started off, thanking God for a safe trip from Detroit to DC to be with us and asking Him to give what she called "traveling mercies" for her trip back. Shontessa showed off, of course. "Thank you, God, for the new Apple Watch that Santa's going to bring me."

It was excruciating to sit and listen to each person talk, while the aroma of the roasted turkey was talking to my stomach and the whiff of the stuffing was making my mouth water and the smell of the pie that was warming in the oven was whispering in my ear, *Hurry up and eat me. You know I'm going to be scrumptious!*

Now, I can list a zillion things in my life that are awesome. But back on *that* Thanksgiving Day, it would've taken me a while to come up with anything. So when it was my turn to speak, my mouth spilled out with what was on my mind before I could stop myself. I said, "I thank God for the baby sister He's going to bless my family with for Christmas."

Daddy gaped at Mom. Mom had tried to take a sip of water and sputtered on it. Uncle Jimmy started grinning and stuck an elbow into Aunt Juicy's rib. Cousin Julia raced out the kitchen holding a dripping spoon high like a baton and said, "Lord Jesus! Sherry, you sure did keep that a secret!" Everybody else in the room was wearing expressions that said, *OMG.*

"I am not having a baby!" Mom finally got out. Then she turned to me. "Jayla, where did you get the crazy idea that I was having a baby?"

"I just want something exciting to happen. A baby would make our family more interesting."

"Would you find changing dirty diapers, wiping spit-up off your shirt, or trying to calm a crying infant *interesting*?" Cousin Julia said, arching her eyebrow as she stared me down.

"Well, it would be different..." But as I thought about it, maybe not different in a way I would like.

"Where do these kids get these ideas from?" Mom said.

"They spend too much time on the Internet," said Cousin Julia.

"They need to play outdoors instead," said Aunt Crystal.

"Yeah, didn't we have fun? Remember how we used to play kickball?" said Uncle Jimmy.

"My favorite was hide-and-go-seek," said Aunt Juicy.

"What about tag? Juicy, you were always It." My mother started laughing as she reminisced.

"I'm sure you all are having a good time walking down memory lane, but how about we finish giving thanks so we can eat?" Daddy said. "Jayla, maybe this time you can say something more appropriate."

So I said, "I thank God for everybody who is here for Thanksgiving."

———

I really did love my family. It just seemed like everything they said and did was the same-old, twice-told stuff they had said and done before. Like every year my mother and her sister, my Aunt Crystal, said they were going to go on a diet. And then they would dig into the cornbread dressing and the sweet potato pie and the wine that was going around the table.

My mom used to be real skinny. I've seen pictures of her when she was in high school. People say we look alike, but I'm short for a fifth grader and my legs are skinny. Daddy describes Mom's complexion as maple syrup and says I'm cinnamon toast; he teases us by saying, "Between the two of you, if I just add a slab of bacon, I've got breakfast." Mom used to wear short, short skirts and had long, strong legs. Sometimes now, she would huff and puff when she came up the stairs with grocery bags. I remember one time we had to run for the bus. We caught it, but when we got on and sat down, she was so out of breath she couldn't speak for a minute. And when she did speak, she said, "You wouldn't believe I used to be the fastest girl in my class, would you?" I wonder what happens to people once they grow up that makes them stop being fast or thin or interesting or fun. It scared me to think about what could happen once you got older. Would I end up slow and thick and dull and dreary when I grew up, too?

After the last person gave thanks, there was a moment of silence. That's when a faint *slap-slap* sound could be heard, followed by cheering.

6

"What's that noise?" somebody said.

Everybody started looking at everybody else, and eventually all eyes landed on Shontessa. The noise was coming from her direction. The adults threw questions at her like she was a bull's-eye.

"What are you looking at?"

"I bet it's her phone."

"What's on that phone that's got your eyes on lockdown?"

"A Double Dutch team," Shontessa answered.

Double Dutch—what was that? It seemed like I had heard the words before, but I couldn't remember where.

"Now that really takes me back," Mom said. She sat up a little straighter. If she had been a puppy, her tail would have been wagging.

"Kids don't play games like that anymore," Uncle Jimmy said. "They can't move like we used to."

"*I* can't move like we used to," Aunt Crystal said with a laugh.

"Crystal, remember how much time we spent doing Double Dutch?" said Aunt Juicy. "Hours and hours. We barely came in the house to eat."

"What exactly is Double Dutch?" I asked. But they were so caught up in their excitement they didn't hear me.

"It was you and Sherry who did it the most," said Aunt Crystal.

"I remember thinking Double Dutch was a lame game for girls. Then I tried it and it nearly killed me," said Uncle Jimmy. "You got to be strong to do that. It ain't no joke."

"Mom, what is—"

"Oh, you smell that? We better get the turkey out of the oven. It's done!"

And with that Mom ran into the kitchen to save the turkey and everybody else filed into the dining room. The conversation then drifted to other topics, while the cooks finished fixing the food and setting the table. After a moment of excitement, it seemed like this was going to turn into just another ho-hum, humdrum Thanksgiving.

Yet now when I look back on it, I see it was that dull Thanksgiving Day that changed my family's life.

CHAPTER 2

That year, we were at Cousin Julia's house for Thanksgiving dinner. I liked my cousin Julia, but boy, was she old. She wasn't the oldest of the old people in my mother's family, but she sure acted like it. Her television wasn't a flat screen; it had a big hump coming out its back. She didn't even have cable. Until I was seven years old, she had a telephone that you had to dial by putting your fingers into holes and turning it in a circle. It would make a *clackety-clack* sound as you dialed the numbers. I kind of liked playing with her phone, but anytime Mom caught me touching it, she would make me stop. Now, Cousin Julia had phones that were not as old-fashioned, but they had long cords that plugged into the wall. She said she had a cell phone, but it was one that was given to her by her job. She always left it at the office at the end of the day because she said she didn't want to work when she was at home.

Talking on the phone wasn't work; it was fun. I wished my school would give everyone phones to take home instead of books. I couldn't wait till Mom thought I was old enough to have my own phone.

Cousin Julia's favorite thing to talk about was her grandchildren. Her son had four kids. They lived in Seattle, Washington, which was a long way from Washington, DC, where we lived.

"Is Washington, DC, the opposite of the state of Washington?" Antwon asked.

"How can a city be the opposite of something?" I said to him. "That doesn't even make sense."

"City is the opposite of country," Shontessa shot back. Who asked her to butt in?

"No, it isn't," I said. "A city is part of a country."

Because they lived so far away, Cousin Julia didn't get to see her grandkids that much. Every Thanksgiving, they called her, and we had to listen to her baby-talk with all her grandbabies and even with her big old son, Ronnie. I'd never met the grandbabies, but I felt like I knew everything about them because she talked about them so much.

Cousin Julia lived in the Hillcrest section of DC, the neighborhood my family lived in. She lived on Pennsylvania

Avenue, which is the same street the president lives on, but Cousin Julia's house was at the opposite end of the city from the White House. The White House is in northwest and Hillcrest is in southeast DC. I think Hillcrest is prettier than the downtown area around the White House. Downtown is asphalt and office buildings. Our neighborhood has lots of large, leafy trees, all kinds of homes—brick houses, town houses, apartments—and hills. I guess that's why they called it Hillcrest.

Cousin Julia's house was big. It had a lot of nooks and crannies. When I was little, I liked to play hide-and-seek in it. Now Tommy and Kwame did. Today they were pretending to be cave explorers. Instead of walking around on their feet like normal people, they were on their hands and knees, crawling under things. "Look what I found!" Tommy was clutching a long, loopy coil of cords going into the wall by the sofa. "Spaghetti!"

"Don't you dare try to eat that," I scolded him.

"We're not going to eat them. They're going to eat you—they're snakes!" Kwame said and shook them at my face while they both fell out laughing.

Cousin Julia's furniture was a mix of old stuff and new stuff. Her sofa was chubby and green with huge, flouncy cushions, but the chairs were the same shiny, silver ones I've seen on one of those TV shows where they redecorate somebody's whole house during the commercial. She had a digital clock in the kitchen but an antique clock in the dining room. Even though the dining room was big, not all thirteen of us could fit around the table. Some people had to take their plates and sit in the living room.

But we did all crowd into the dining room for grace. There was Mom and Daddy, of course. Daddy looked like he couldn't wait to eat. He was craning his neck like he was trying to see when the food was coming out. I saw that Aunt Elizabeth, Shontessa's mother, was wearing a hat, which was good because she always seemed to be having a bad hair day. Aunt Crystal was standing next to Cousin Eddie, who was standing next to Uncle Jimmy, who had a heavy hand clamped to one shoulder each of Tommy and Kwame. It kept them from squirming away, although it didn't stop them from squirming. The cooks were standing in the doorway to the kitchen. Usually, one of the adults was called on to lead the prayer, but this year, Aunt Crystal spoke up.

"Let Antwon say the grace," she said. "He prayed in front of the whole Sunday school last week and did real good."

Antwon was off in a corner with Shontessa, and Aunt Crystal had to call him several times to get him to come out. I could never get up in front of a whole bunch of people, even if it was only my family and I knew everybody. At least if you mess up in front of strangers, you'll never see them again. Mess up in front of family and they'll talk about it forever. I could just imagine the gossip:

"You remember that Thanksgiving when Jayla flubbed up the prayer big time?"

"Yeah, girl! She was supposed to be praying over the food. Instead we had to pray over her."

"Dear God," Antwon said. "We thank You for this food we are about to receive and we thank You for the miracles You are about to perform. Amen."

I wondered how it is that someone as slow as Antwon was brave enough to stand up in public. Was it because he was so clueless? Or did he know something I didn't know? Whatever it was, I wished I had it.

Then instead of sitting down at the table or getting himself a plate, he and Shontessa ran back off to a corner of the hallway and were looking at something on her phone screen.

"What's got you so caught up?" asked Uncle Jimmy. Shontessa thrust her cell phone at him to show him the YouTube video they were watching. I leaned over her shoulder so I could see, too. It was four girls jumping rope but doing it a way I had never seen before.

"Look at her jump!" I said. "She's doing two ropes at the same time! How can she do that?"

"Man, that ain't no big deal," Uncle Jimmy said. "Your

mama used to do that all the time. Heck, I even got in the rope every now and then."

"No, you all didn't," I said. Uncle Jimmy is known for his tall tales.

"Yes, we did, too. Your mother loved jumping Double Dutch. Did it all the time."

"Mom, is that true?"

My mom wasn't paying any attention to me.

"Mom!" I yelled louder. "Can you jump Double Dutch?"

"Hush that noise, yelling like a girl from the projects." Mom stuck her head out the kitchen. "Yes, I can jump Double Dutch."

"You can jump like them?" I showed her the screen. There were two girls on the screen jumping in rhythm while doing a chant. At one point, they changed positions—the one in front moved back and the one in back moved to the front. How could they do that without missing a beat?

"Your mother used to do nothing but jump Double Dutch all day long," said Juicy. Aunt Juicy is my mother's baby sister. She got her nickname because of her lips. Aunt Juicy now lives in Detroit, but most holidays she comes back to DC. "Not only could she jump, she could do tricks in the rope."

"Really! Let me see."

"You won't see nothing. We've got food to eat." Mom

rearranged some of the dishes on the table to make more room for the food she was about to bring out.

"The food'll wait. Let me see you jump."

"I know how to jump rope," Shontessa said, butting into the conversation. "I have a rope at home that lights up."

"I'm not talking about jumping single. I'm talking about Double Dutch."

"I bet I could do that, too," said Shontessa.

"But you couldn't do it like Sherry," said Aunt Juicy. "She was the captain of her Double Dutch squad."

"Girl, go on," my mother said, waving her hand at Juicy like she was shooing away someone who was smoking too close to her face. But then she started grinning and said, "I wasn't the captain. I was the queen."

I was about to ask Mom to tell me more, but she ducked back in the kitchen, and when she came out again, she was carrying the turkey and Aunt Juicy was carrying a pan in each hand and set them on the table like she was putting jewels on display. The sweet potatoes were a warm golden color. The cranberry sauce was as shiny as if it had been polished before being put on the plate. The turkey sat in the center of the table like a big, bronze crown—until we cut it up, ate it up, and it became a bony memory. Everybody was quiet for a moment as folks dug into the good food. I was the first one to break the silence.

"Let me see you jump Double Dutch, Mom. Show me how you did it."

"I'm trying to eat, Jayla."

"C'mon, Mom, I wanna see you jump Double Dutch!"

"Well, I can't very well jump in here. Even if I did, I'd break every chair, lamp, and table."

"Let's go outside."

"We'll catch our deaths outside. Don't you know it's November?"

This was when I wished I had siblings; they'd go outside with me to play.

"It's not that cold, and it's still light outside," I told her.

We had started Thanksgiving dinner at lunchtime. Or rather a very late lunch. We sat down at the table around 3:30 and it was now about 4:15 p.m. So there was still some daylight. And although there was no mistaking the day for warm, the temperature was chilly in a friendly way. Just cold enough to need a jacket but not so cold as to make you shiver.

"I would probably break both my legs."

"Don't hurt your legs. When my knees start acting up, all I can do is go somewhere and sit down." That was from Aunt Crystal who complained whenever she had to walk more than three steps in a row. That turned the conversation to talk about medical bills and all the aches and pains that old folks always talk about.

Shontessa caught my eye and she said, "Wanna see something cool?" She was sitting two people down the table from me. I nodded and she passed me her phone. It was another team of Double Dutch girls. This video showed one girl who jumped up high and came back down right in step and on beat. Then the other girl did a jump with her legs spread wide and *she* came back down right in step and on beat. It was like they were jumping, marching, and dancing all at the same time.

"*Wow!* That is so cool!" I said. It came out before I could stop myself. My outburst interrupted Aunt Juicy, who had been talking about a fire that had burned out several families in Detroit. It seemed like I was saying it was cool that these people had just lost their homes. Juicy gave me a nasty glare, and Mom snapped at me. "What are you looking at?"

"More Double Dutch." I passed the phone to her so she could see. "Mom, can you high-jump like that?"

"That's called a pop up. And, yes, I can. When I was your age, I could do that and more."

"Put that away, please," said Cousin Julia. "No cell phones at my dinner table. We're here to be with each other, not with some idiots on YouTube."

"You'd talk on the phone if your grandkids called on the landline," I protested. "Why can't I look at something on Shontessa's phone?"

"Jayla, that's enough," said Daddy. I shut up, but I didn't think it was fair.

"Sherry, you and Julia tore it up for Thanksgiving this year!" said Aunt Crystal. "Everything is delicious. If there are any leftovers, I'm taking them home."

"Next year, we're going to put you in the kitchen," joked my mother. Everybody knew her sister Crystal couldn't cook.

"Even if I knew how to cook, I wouldn't have the time." Aunt Crystal worked as a pharmacist for a drugstore chain. She was on duty at night and got home late most evenings.

"Julia, how's Ronnie and his kids doing?" asked Cousin Eddie. I never was sure who Cousin Eddie was related to, but he showed up every Thanksgiving.

"Fine, last time we talked. His oldest son just got a scholarship to Sunderland Prep, so he'll be starting sixth grade at a private school. The middle boy has started playing oboe."

"The *oboe*? Why *that*, of all musical instruments?" said Cousin Eddie. "He should be playing something loud and proud—the drums or the trumpet, something like that."

Cousin Julia ignored Cousin Eddie and kept rolling on about how wonderful her grandkids were.

"And the baby is just as cute as a button. Did you see the latest picture?" She went to the bookcase and actually pulled out a photo album. She's the only person I know who keeps pictures in a book. Everybody else I know keeps their pictures on their phone.

"You know they phone me every Thanksgiving. What time is it? They've usually called by now. We'll probably hear from them in a few minutes."

"I know you're proud of those boys," said Aunt Crystal.

"Yes, I am. Sometimes I wasn't sure if Ronnie was going to make it, but he finally got himself together and has become a great father." Cousin Julia flipped through the album, stopping now and then to smile at one of the pictures of her grandchildren as if they could see her beaming at them. "Thank the Lord."

"Ronnie was a fool to have so many children. It sounds like his children got more sense than him," said Uncle Jimmy.

It was funny to me that Uncle Jimmy called Ronnie a fool, since Uncle Jimmy couldn't control his own children. Kwame and Tommy were just about the craziest kids I'd ever seen. But at least those kids had each other. I was all by myself.

Big Lucy jumped into the conversation with a statement that I thought was so true it should be added to the Bible. "Just because you're young, it doesn't mean you're stupid. And just because you're old, it doesn't mean you're smart."

"But some people are stupid at every age," Daddy said.

Like Antwon. Antwon was only eleven, but I was afraid he might stay stupid his whole life.

"There are different kinds of intelligence," said Aunt Crystal. "Some people have book knowledge; some people are artistic. And athletes are smart in a yet another way."

"Sherry is smart in a couple of different ways," said Daddy. "She's a good cook, and she has book smarts."

"And she was the LeBron James of jump rope," said Aunt Juicy. "The Beyoncé of Double Dutch. Too bad she couldn't have gone to college on a Double Dutch scholarship."

"Yeah, that would have saved me years of paying student loans," Mom said.

My mother, the Beyoncé of Double Dutch? She must have been stupendous. After that, I *had* to see it with my own eyes. I begged and begged my mother to jump. I replayed the YouTube video all through dessert. After dinner, when the grown-ups started drifting to the TV, I had Shontessa's phone out and kept asking my mother if she could jump like *this* girl or do the same tricks as *that* jumper.

Hearing us talking about jumping made Tommy and Kwame start jumping up and down everywhere. Kwame sat his butt on a chair with a pot-bellied cushion and started bouncing. Then Tommy stood up on the sofa and treated it like a trampoline. Finally, when Tommy climbed up on the coffee table and began to shout, "Geronimo!" Uncle Jimmy grabbed him and Kwame and told them to go outside and burn off some of that energy.

"I could use some fresh air myself," said my mother. "It was hot in that kitchen."

"You got that right. I'm right behind you, girl." Juicy joined my mother leaving the house.

I followed her into the front yard while Uncle Jimmy took Tommy-and-Kwame-the-Human-Tsunami out back. As we headed out, I saw Shontessa putting on her sweater as if she was planning to go outdoors, too. I was praying she'd follow Tommy and Kwame and them, but no, she followed us.

"Aunt Sherry, were you really good at Double Dutch like the girls in the video?" she asked.

"Yes, I was and I'm not bragging."

"Let us see you jump! Pleeeease!" I said for the twenty-millionth time.

"Girl, you won't let it rest, will you? Even if I wanted to do it, I have no rope."

"Back in the day, we used a clothesline," said Juicy.

"A clothesline? What do you mean? You tied your clothes together end to end and used them as a rope? How did that work?" This was from Antwon, who had come outside looking for Tommy and Kwame.

"No, a clothesline was a rope used for hanging up clothes to dry outside. You pinned the clothes to the line and the air dried them. Hence, clothesline."

That sounded like something cavewomen would do. But

we were getting away from the subject. And before I could get back on the subject, Kwame and Tommy came tearing around the side of the house from the backyard. *Oh no.* If Kwame and Tommy were with us, they would do something to irritate the grown-ups and we'd all be sent back into the house and I'd lose my chance to convince my mother to show me her Double Dutch moves.

"I won!" Tommy cried out. "I beat you!"

"You should have another race," I suggested. "Let's see who can run the fastest back to where you were."

"No, I'm tired. And cold!" Kwame was hugging his arms in close and shivered a bit. "I'll beat you the next time. I just let you win this time."

"Go inside and get your jacket off the bed," Uncle Jimmy told Kwame.

"What do you mean, the bed?" asked Kwame.

"Jayla, go with him so he doesn't treat the mattress like a launching pad," Uncle Jimmy said. Kwame and I headed into the house. All the coats were stacked up in the master bedroom, making a colossal heap on the bed. It looked like a sleeping animal with a multicolored hide. Someone's sweater felt like a soft pillow. I wanted to lie down on it and feel it caress my cheek. We dug through a scratchy plaid jacket and a black leather coat. Finally, we pulled out Kwame's hoodie and headed back out.

"I bet you could use this for a jump rope." Kwame stopped by the foot of the sofa and picked up a coil.

"What is that?"

"I was going to use it to lasso Tommy. It's my cowboy rope. But I'll let you jump with it."

Great! Now Mom had no excuse. Here was a rope; well, a cowboy rope, not a Double Dutch rope, but I figured she could make it work.

"Hey, Mom—now can I see you jump?" I called out, holding the rope.

"We're in business now!" squealed Juicy, and she ran over and uncoiled it. She took one end and Mom took the other, then doubled it, so they each had two ends in hand. Then they started turning.

Phwap. Phwap. The slap of the plastic cords was that same rhythm I had seen in the video. And the movement of the ropes was the same circles sweeping over and under, over and under. Watching it made me feel hypnotized.

"Who left the door open?" Cousin Julia stood in the doorway. "You're letting the heat escape. That's like throwing money out the—" And then she stopped talking as she took in what she was seeing. Mom and Juicy turning Double Dutch with two big arcs hitting the front sidewalk like gentle drumbeats. It was almost magnetic, how the rhythm pulled you into its spell.

"Double Dutch! Chile, I haven't seen anybody do that in a hundred years." And with no more warning than that, Cousin Julia jumped into the rope and was going for it. Soon she was jumping and chanting:

"I like coffee. I like tea. I like the boys and the boys like me. A. B. C. D. E…" She kept going till she missed on the letter M.

"Who's your secret boyfriend whose name begins with M?" teased Juicy.

"His name ought to be Mr. Money," snapped Cousin Julia. "Where'd you find a rope?"

Kwame piped up. "From the telephone."

"From the telephone?" She stopped, picked up the cord, and took a closer look at it.

"What! You boys unplugged my phone? No wonder my grandbabies didn't call me. What's wrong with you? Jimmy, get these fool boys out of my sight before I go off on both of them and you right along with them. Tearing up my stuff. I talk to my grandbabies every Thanksgiving, and I was wondering why I hadn't heard from them. Not only did you disconnect the phone, but you tricked me into shredding my own phone cord to pieces!"

Mom and Juicy had dropped the rope, and Cousin Julia rolled it up around her arm as she continued fussing. I just stood there with my mouth hanging open, taking in all that had just happened.

My mother could jump Double Dutch. My Uncle Jimmy said he could jump Double Dutch. Even old Cousin Julia could jump Double Dutch.

I wanted to jump, too.

CHAPTER 3

There was a place right on my butt where I had an itch, but I couldn't scratch because I was in church, wedged in tight between my mom and Cousin Julia among ten people in a row meant for eight. I tried to hit the itch by wiggling in my seat, but Mom hissed, "Stop that squirming."

I made myself sit still, but I scooted my hand below my waistband and managed to scratch out a little relief.

"What are you doing?" whispered Cousin Julia when my elbow poked her.

"Sorry," I mumbled and tried not to move anymore.

It was the Sunday after Thanksgiving, and church was packed. A lot of people had family in town and lots of them had all come to church together. There were two families in attendance with someone from each generation: grandmother,

mother, and teens and kids. There were several single people, mostly women my mom's age and older. One group was a father with three little boys; they were wiggle worms. I bet they were a lot like Tommy and Kwame. The difference was that when this father gave them *that look*, they settled down.

"This is the day the Lord has made. Let us rejoice and be glad in it!" said Deacon Tom. "Would the visitors please stand?" Lots of family groups stood up. *Do all those people like each other?* I wondered. *Do they get along? Did they enjoy Thanksgiving dinner, or did they muddle through it like I had? Is there a Shontessa in every group, or do other families know how to make family members act right?*

One family caught my attention. I knew they were visitors, although they didn't stand up to be recognized. It was a mother and her daughter. The girl looked like she was one or two years younger than me. I guessed they didn't stand because they didn't want to draw attention to themselves.

It's funny how church is such a quiet place even though there are plenty of sounds around. People praying and praising, pastor preaching, and, of course, lots of music.

It didn't seem to matter that some folks didn't look—or act—so nice. Like the boy whose necktie was lopsided, or the woman who nodded off and snored a little, or the usher whose suit was wrinkled—somehow it was all okay. When it was time to sing, everyone's voices blended together. Even when I could hear the sound of someone whose voice wasn't that great, it still worked. Not because they sounded good but because everyone got to be part of the music.

After we sang the last hymn, I was eager to get going. Mom, Cousin Julia, and I were planning to go to the mall right after service. But they were hanging around talking and talking.

"I couldn't believe she did that. Right in the middle of service." Cousin Julia was outraged. I wondered what had happened that got her so upset. I was sitting right beside her in church and I didn't remember anything outrageous happening.

"She probably just forgot to turn off her cell. I'm sure she didn't intend to be disruptive," Mom said. Now I knew what Cousin Julia was talking about.

Shortly after the sermon started, a phone rang. The ringtone repeated several times because the phone's owner didn't realize it was hers at first. It turned out it belonged to the lady who hadn't stood up during the welcome. When she realized it was her phone, she softly said hello, stood up, and walked out the sanctuary, whispering on the phone.

"But why are you so mad, Cousin Julia?" I asked. "How is that any different from a baby crying and the mom or dad whispering to calm it down and then stepping outside?"

And as if on cue, Sister Arora walked up to us to say hello and her baby started crying. Loud.

29

"Aw…why is the itty-bitty baby crying?" cooed Cousin Julia and moved closer to them.

Cousin Julia was smiling at the baby like he was something sweet to eat. The baby was way noisier than the ringtone, but Cousin Julia wasn't upset with the baby. I didn't get it. She was trying to make the baby happy and was trying to make the mother feel better. Yet she talked about the lady with the cell phone like she was a criminal.

I looked around. I saw the lady with the phone. She was just standing with her little girl near the church bulletin board, looking a bit lost. Deacon Tom was slapping Brother Shelton on the back. Three women were huddled together having a heated conversation while passing a brochure back and forth between them. A boy was standing by her looking at the same bulletin board. There were conversations going on all around her, but nobody was talking to her. I walked over.

"Hi," I said. "Is this your first time at our church?"

"Yes, I'm in town visiting my brother who lives in the neighborhood," she said. "I thought I'd come out to this church since it was nearby."

"Well, welcome. My name is Jayla."

"I'm Ms. Miner, and this is my daughter, Maya."

Maya. I used to have a best friend named Maya, but she moved away last year after fourth grade when her father got a job in Atlanta. It made me sad for a minute, thinking of Maya. But I didn't let myself keep thinking about it. I just said, "That's a pretty name. I like it."

Maya smiled and her mother looked pretty pleased, too.

"I think I might've crossed a line when my phone rang during service," Ms. Miner said.

"Oh, don't worry about it," I reassured her. "It's okay. All you missed was a boring part of the sermon."

"Told ya," Maya said.

"You're very sweet to say hello to us," Ms. Miner said. "Next time we're in DC, we're going to come back to this church just to see you!"

They headed out, and I went back to where my family was still standing, still talking away.

"They grow so fast!" Mom said to the new mother. "I remember back at the church health fair last June, you were still pregnant. Now you have a pretty baby *and* you've gotten your figure back!"

"I'm jealous!" Cousin Julia said good-naturedly. She played with the baby's toes.

"Well, it wasn't easy," Sister Arora said. "At the health fair, one of the nurses told me not to stop exercising after the baby arrived. It's been hard, but I've managed to squeeze it in."

"It was at the health fair that a lady from the health department told me I was borderline," Mom said to Sister

Arora. I recalled when the nurse had put Mom's arm in a wrapper that pumped up with air while watching a clocklike meter. "You'll need to change your diet and start exercising," the nurse had told her.

"I have time to eat but not to exercise," my mother had quipped and laughed with the nurse, then left the booth. "My goal back in June at the health fair was to lose fifteen pounds. Now, I only have twenty more to go!" joked Mom. "I'd love to look like her." She tilted her head toward a woman who had just passed by.

"She looks like Mary Mack," said Cousin Julia.

"Who's Mary Mack?" my mother asked. I turned to see who they were talking about. Mom and Cousin Julia were looking at a lady standing by the water fountain. She was real tall and skinny and had on a black body-hugging dress. It had those decorations on the shoulders that soldiers in uniform wear, silver and fringy. A row of matching buttons traveled from the back of her neck to her waist.

"'Miss Mary Mack, all dressed in black,' don't you remember?" Cousin Julia said.

"Yeah, she does look like she could be Miss Mary Mack," agreed my mother.

"Who is Miss Mary Mack?" I asked, now curious. She must be pretty stylish. The woman they were talking about had on high heels and a fat silver ring on her finger. The shoes were black with a silver design on them. Everything matched.

"She asked her mother for fifteen cents," Cousin Julia said in a singsong voice. Why would this Mary Mack person ask her mother for fifteen cents? What could you do with only fifteen cents?

"To see the elephant jump over the fence," my mother answered back in the same singsong rhythm.

Okay, I saw that it was some sort of rap. Then they both started singing it at the same time.

"He jumped so high, high, high, he touched the sky, sky, sky, and he never came back, back, back till the Fourth of July-ly-ly!"

Cousin Julia and my mother laughed together but what tripped me out was that the lady in black turned around when she heard them chanting and joined in with them.

"I guess this *is* a Miss Mary Mack kind of outfit," the lady said.

"What's with Miss Mary Mack?" I persisted.

"Oh, it's just an old rhyme we used to recite sometimes when doing hand-clapping games or Double Dutch," Cousin Julia said.

"Double Dutch?" My ears perked up. "You're going to do Double Dutch?"

"Wouldn't that be whack?" said Miss Mary Mack's twin. "I always wanted to learn Double Dutch."

"They could teach you," I said excitedly. Maybe Cousin Julia and my mother could do a quick demonstration and I'd get to see my mother in action.

"We used to do it back in the day, but I wouldn't dare do it now," my mother said.

"Why not? There's enough space." I gestured to the wide hallway that had people in it five deep.

"Not as big as I am now," said my mother.

"What does that have to do with it? You're not *that* big. If an elephant could jump over a fence, you could probably jump over a rope."

Cousin Julia and the Miss Mary Mack lady cracked up, but my mother's frown was fixed on her face with superglue.

"Not at church, Jayla. Really?"

"And not in these heels," Miss Mary Mack laughed. Miss Mary Mack wandered off while we were still in the church vestibule chatting with other people. But I could tell Mom hadn't gotten over being ticked off with me because the plans to go Christmas shopping changed. Mom snapped out her phone and made a call, then told me I wouldn't be going with them.

I tried to persuade her. "I wanted to pick out some stuff for Christmas. There's lots of stuff on sale."

But she wasn't budging. "I need some time just with grown-ups," she said. "Case closed."

Instead, they were going to drop me off for a last-minute Niece Night. Niece Night wasn't actually a nighttime thing. It meant I was going to be spending Sunday afternoon at my cousin Alonzo's house.

It was probably more fun to go to Alonzo's house anyway. Cousin Alonzo was my coolest cousin. He was my father's nephew and my favorite grown-up. He didn't have any children, so he usually spoiled me. He would take me and the other kids in the family to cool places like the yearly auto show or a black history program. Niece Night was something that had gotten started when Alonzo was a kid. Then, it was Nephew Night. His Uncle Javon would take Alonzo and all his other nephews and they'd hang out, go to a basketball game or something like that. Then Daddy's sister, Aunt Stacie, had said, "What about the girls?" So then they started Niece Night. Alonzo kept it up, even after he got grown. He would call me up and say something like, "It's about time we had a Niece Night." Or even a Niece and Nephew Night. And he'd get a bunch of kids—it didn't have to be real nieces and nephews, just whoever was able to hang out or whose parents wanted their kids out of the house—and we'd have a get together. A lot of times, we didn't even go anywhere. We'd just go to Alonzo's house and eat.

Everybody in my family had a way of getting under my skin, but Cousin Alonzo was always cool with me.

"Hi, Cousin Alonzo! What are we going to do for Niece

Night today?" I ran into the living room of his place. He had the largest music and video collection of anybody I knew. In addition to streaming songs on his iPhone, he had an MP3 player, a CD player, and a record player. A huge TV was mounted on the wall of his living room.

"Hey, Jayla-Jayla. We'll do whatever you want to do. TV, video games, cards, total world takeover—you name it!"

Hmmm…I thought I might be in a video game mood. There was this new game, *ShoutOut*, that nobody I knew had gotten other than Alonzo. And Shontessa.

"How about *ShoutOut*?" I said. Alonzo didn't answer. While I was thinking about what to do, he'd pulled out his phone. "How about *ShoutOut*?" I tried again.

"Huh?" Alonzo's mind was far away from me. He was looking at his phone like there was something important happening on his screen. I waited for a minute but he didn't say anything else.

"Alonzo, are we going to play *ShoutOut*?"

"If you want to, go ahead," Alonzo said, gesturing toward the TV. I went ahead and got started, but it wasn't fun if he wasn't playing. In fact, the whole visit wasn't feeling like much fun at all.

"The last time I played this game, Shontessa won, but I think she cheated," I shared, and waited for Alonzo to say something to make me feel better.

"You and that Shontessa always be bumping heads," Alonzo said without looking up.

"What are you looking at on your phone?"

"Just texting something to my friend."

"About what?"

"I'm winding it up now. So what are you playing?"

It was obvious he wasn't really interested in playing the video game. Maybe I could get him to talk.

"Can I ask you something?"

"Sure, Jayla-Jayla. What you want to know?"

"Do you like everyone in your whole family? Don't they get on your nerves someti—"

His phone rang.

"Hey, baby," Alonzo said into his cell. "What you got for me?" He was grinning big as he listened to the person on the other end of the conversation. It was like he smiled with his whole body—he stood much taller yet looked way more relaxed all at the same time. "Yeah, that sounds good."

Then he walked into the bedroom and shut the door. Good grief, what was so secret he had to leave the room? Alonzo was gone for what felt like a long time; I finished the game waiting for him. This was definitely no fun. This was an extremely negative Niece Night.

When he came out, he was still wearing a slight smile. Whoever he was talking to must really make him feel happy.

"When are we going to play, Cousin Alonzo?" I knew I was whining, but he hadn't spent any real time with me.

"Okay, let's get this party started," he said. "You want something to eat?"

That sounded good. I hadn't eaten anything since breakfast. Maybe he would cook something or even take me out to eat. "Yes, please!" I said.

"Here, catch." He threw me a bag of Krazy Krunchies. I love Krazy Krunchies— they're sweet and salty, and once you start, you can't stop—but I was expecting more than just a snack in a sack.

"Aren't you going to fix anything else to eat?" Alonzo liked to cook, and he usually had good food at his house.

"Didn't you eat before you came? I'm sorry but I didn't fix anything 'cause I didn't know you were coming in advance and I'm going out to eat later, as soon as you leave."

"Can't I go out to eat with you?"

"Nah, I'm hanging out with a grown-up friend. Next time, Jayla."

It seemed like today all the grown-ups wanted to X me out. For Christmas, I had planned to ask for few video games. But I was starting to think I should ask for an app to reboot and update my family.

CHAPTER 4

Christmas at my house was a lot more fun than Thanksgiving. Usually we opened gifts at dinner on Christmas Eve, and then on Christmas morning, we went to church. Christmas dinner was spent with Daddy's side of the family. His people weren't as prickly and exhausting as Mom's family. Mom's relatives were like trying to eat a peanut butter sandwich without the jelly: tasty but hard to chew. Daddy's people were like strawberry smoothies; they went down easy.

That year, dinner was at Cousin Alonzo's. Even though he had kinda ignored me the last time I visited, I couldn't stay mad at him. Cousin Alonzo was really cute and every year he had a different girlfriend with him for Christmas. Two years ago, he had a girlfriend named Aisha who looked like a model. The year before her was a woman with the longest, most glamorous weave I'd ever seen. Her name was Aisha, too. Different women, same name. Last Christmas, the girl had been a lady with a curly Afro named Tameka.

I was always curious to see what Alonzo's girlfriends wore. Alonzo liked to dress sharp, and he liked women who could dress too. The year of the first Aisha, she wore skyscraper stilettos with red soles. The year of the second Aisha, she wore a winter white sweater with fur around the sleeves and the collar. She said it was real mink but I think she might have been teasing me.

Last year's girlfriend, Tameka, wasn't dressed as fancy as the previous women. I couldn't even remember what she had on. So I was especially looking forward to seeing what Alonzo's latest lady would be wearing.

When me, Mom, and Daddy got to Alonzo's front door, he opened it wide and his smile was even wider.

"Ho, ho, ho," he bellowed. "Merry Christmas to my favorite peeps!"

He said that to everyone when they came in, but, you know, I think he meant it just the same.

"And how's my favorite girl?" This was said to me. And I *know* he meant it where I was concerned.

"Y'all remember Tameka, don't you?"

Tameka? Wasn't that the same girl who came last year? Coming around the corner was a brown-skinned woman with a curly Afro wearing a Christmas sweater—an ugly one—and boring blue jeans. She was almost as tall as Alonzo.

"Jayla, right?"

Wow. She remembered my name.

"Yes, how are you? Merry Christmas." I wondered how such a plain Jane managed to get a second invitation from Cousin Alonzo. She gave me a hug, and I noticed she smelled pretty.

"I like your perfume."

"Oh, thank you. You're probably smelling grease and gravy; I've been cooking," she said, laughing. "Although by the smell coming from the kitchen, I think my sweet potatoes are ready."

She hurried off, and we sat down in the living room with the others.

"What you been doing for yourself?" my dad said to Alonzo.

"Working. That's about all."

"Knowing you, you're not working hard—you're hardly working."

"Their salary is a joke, so I laugh when they ask me to do something."

The grown-ups laughed. Alonzo always makes everyone laugh. He's a lot of fun to be around. I know Christmas is supposed to be a holiday to honor the birth of Jesus and

Thanksgiving is to show how grateful we are for everything, but there should be a holiday just for laughing. If there was such a holiday, Alonzo would be its king.

Pretty soon everyone was sitting down to eat. Tameka set the sweet potatoes down in front of me, so I was the first person to dig into them. My nose took in their cinnamon sweetness promising yumminess and my tongue was not disappointed. I also piled on macaroni and cheese. I was surprised when Mom passed the platter of mac and cheese on to Alonzo without taking any. Macaroni and cheese was Alonzo's special dish. He made it with three cheeses. Let me see if I can remember their names: Romano, Parmesan, and cheddar. Not only was he fun to hang out with, but he could cook, too.

Then there was chocolate cake, sweet potato pie, and that multicolored ice cream divided into three. I could never remember what you call that ice cream. All I knew was I liked it. But before Alonzo served the dessert, he tapped on a wineglass and said, "I have something important I want to say."

"You may have cooties, you may have bills, but I seriously doubt you have anything important to say," joked Daddy.

Folks laughed, but only a little bit because they were waiting to hear Alonzo's news.

"You see this beautiful woman right here?" He was gazing at Tameka.

Beautiful? The main thing she had going for her was long legs. Tameka looked okay, but she was no way near as pretty as the Aishas, and she didn't dress all that great, either.

"Well, I asked her to be my wife and she did me the honor of saying yes. I wanted to present her with this engagement ring and formally welcome her to the family."

And then Alonzo brought out a tiny teal-blue box, and when he held it up, someone said, "Whoa, he must be in love 'cause he sure done spent a lot of money."

Tameka took the ring out of the box.

"That thing's so bright it could put out the sun!" That was from Cousin Eddie.

It *was* pretty. Tameka hugged Alonzo, and he turned the hug into a big, showy kiss, and everybody applauded.

"A toast!" Alonzo said, and everybody raised glasses. "Here's to my favorite girl!"

At first, I thought he was saying it to me. But when I saw the way he was looking into Tameka's eyes, I knew he wasn't thinking about me at all.

After dinner, the adults sat around in the dining room talking and teens were in the living room playing video games. The grown-ups' conversation was about bills and sports and whose marriage was falling apart. Some of that was interesting; some of it was not. The kids my age were playing Roblox or Minecraft, and I wasn't in the mood for that. The little kids were parked in a back bedroom watching cartoons. I didn't want to be around babies watching babyfied TV.

My mother and some of the others were in the kitchen, but I didn't want to go in there because they'd make me help clean up. So I sat on the floor where I could catch snatches of the conversation from both the kitchen and the dining room.

"Who do you like for the Super Bowl?"

"As long as it's not the Deadskins, I'm happy."

Cousin Alonzo and Daddy were having their never-ending football fight in the living room. In the kitchen, I overheard, "Girl, those are some cute shoes. You shouldn't leave them lying on the floor."

"Cute but killers. That's why I'm standing at the sink washing dishes in my bare feet."

There was a stray sheet of paper that had floated to the floor, a flyer advertising a Christmas sale. I flipped it over and started doodling.

From the dining room, I heard, "Well, Alonzo, welcome to the world of wedlock. Do you want my advice on marriage?"

"No!"

"Well, I'm going to give it to you anyway. You can disagree with your wife but never on days that begin with T: Tuesday, Thursday, today, tomorrow…"

"Don't talk like that. Tameka looks like a good one. Plus, she can cook!"

"A girl who knows how to cook can always find a man who knows how to eat!"

"Well, I can throw down in the kitchen, too!" I heard Alonzo say. "Anything she can do, I can do better."

Then I heard my father's voice as he weighed in. "Alonzo, the only thing bigger than your appetite is your ego."

Laughter. Then someone lowered his voice and said something else and all the grown-ups really started laughing and talking in low voices.

I turned my attention back to the kitchen. They were talking in lowered tones, too.

"Oh, Sherry. You're going to have to take care of yourself." Aunt Stacie was speaking to my mother. "That's nothing to play with."

"I know, I know. My doctor says I need to exercise," Mom said, agreeing. She was about to say something else, but I couldn't hear it because someone in the dining room said in a loud voice, "I tell you. The first half of my life was ruined by my parents and the second half by my children."

"The thing that keeps me going is my child. I want to stay healthy enough to be there for her." This was my mother speaking again. I started making spiky marks on the page. What was Mom talking about? Her voice sounded very sad and serious.

"You know why Carrie isn't here for Christmas this year? She had a stroke because of her hypertension. You don't want that to happen to you, Sherry."

"I know, I know. I need to take care of myself. It's just hard to find time to work out. And who has money to pay for a gym?"

Did that mean my mother was sick? She didn't look sick. I kept sketching creatures with spiky edges on them. My animals looked like a cross between dogs and dinosaurs.

"Getting married makes you fat," said Mom. "Before I got married, I was slim like you, Tameka. Make sure you continue to work out after you marry."

"I like to exercise," said Tameka. "Sometimes Alonzo and I go on walks together."

Hey! I wanted to shout. Alonzo used to take *me* for walks through the neighborhood. Come to think of it, he hadn't done that with me for months. But evidently, he was walking all over the place with this Tameka.

And once I thought about it, last Christmas, he had let me help out in the kitchen to get dinner ready. He had picked me up from church and brought me to Aunt Stacie's house early. That's when he showed me the three cheeses he had used to make his famous mac and cheese. He had left for a minute to go pick up Tameka and bring her to Aunt Stacie's. I remember because when he left, Aunt Stacie said to me, "He's going to make some woman a good husband."

And I had said, "Cousin Alonzo doesn't need to get married. He's got you and me and Daddy to keep him company."

Aunt Stacie had smiled at me and said, "Yes, family is forever. Even if Alonzo gets married, he won't forget us."

Gone and forgotten—that's what people often said. I hadn't gone anywhere, but I definitely felt forgotten.

CHAPTER 5

Saturdays. I liked Saturdays because I didn't have to go to school. I liked school, but I also liked not having to go. I didn't like Saturdays because, instead of school, I had to do chores. I liked Saturdays because my mother didn't fuss about me playing video games or watching TV because it wasn't a school night. I didn't like Saturdays because sometimes I got tired of playing video games and then I got bored.

I wasn't sure whether or not this was a Saturday I would like. Shontessa's mother had to go to work and had asked if Shontessa could spend the day with us. I had just spent Thanksgiving dinner with her. I wasn't expecting to see Shontessa again till Cousin Julia's Easter dinner. Yet here it was, the Saturday after Christmas, and she was in my face already. But Aunt Elizabeth, Shontessa's mother, had loaded her cash app with money and told her to make sure she spent some of it on me. "Treat the girls to a nice lunch," she had said to Shontessa in front of me and my mother.

"So, what do you want to do?" I asked her.

"Can we go to the mall?"

"You all love to go shopping," Daddy said, sprawled on the couch scrolling through his phone. "Is that the only thing you can think of to do?"

Actually, going to the mall sounded like a great idea to me. Shontessa was wearing some sneakers I had seen worn by some backup dancers in a music video. Maybe she would tell me where she bought them, so I could get a pair, too.

"I've got some Christmas money I need to spend," Shontessa said.

"I've got some Christmas money, too," I told Shontessa.

"I got a whole lot of money for Christmas," she told me.

"Your money is burning a hole in your pocket. You ought to save that money," chided Daddy. He put the phone down to give us his whole attention. Was he going to ruin our Saturday shopping?

"Isn't the purpose of money to spend it?" I said. "What good is it if it just sits around in your wallet doing nothing all day?"

"Yeah, Cousin Keith," Shontessa said, chiming in. "That's

like if you had a nice ripe banana and you kept it for weeks and weeks and never ate it. It would rot and turn nasty. We have to spend our money before it spoils!"

"What are *you* planning to do today, Keith?" Mom asked. She walked in from the kitchen, munching some Krazy Krunchies, and offered him a handful.

"Football! Alonzo is coming over in a little while to watch the game with me."

"Oh, I'd like to see Cousin Alonzo!" I said. I hadn't seen him since Christmas, and the one time I had called him, he was out on a date. If he was coming over to watch sports, he probably wouldn't have Tameka with him. It would be good to be able to talk to him without her around. Maybe I wouldn't have to hang around Shontessa either if I could hang with him. "Is he coming soon?"

"By the time he gets here, you'll be at the mall," Daddy said. "You know when you and your mom start shopping, you can't stop. He'll get here after you leave and will be gone before you get back."

But no sooner had he said that than the doorbell rang. I ran to open the door. It was Cousin Alonzo. Great! I thought about staying home with him and Daddy. Not that I wanted to watch football, but maybe Cousin Alonzo would play a video game or two with me before the game started.

But there was Tameka, right behind him.

"Are you going to let us in, or are you going to let us freeze out here?" Alonzo said good-naturedly. Of course, I let them in, but I would have been happy to freeze Tameka out.

"Hi, Jayla," Tameka said as she came forward. "Happy New Year."

I didn't say anything but opened the door wide, so they could walk through. Alonzo gave me a quick hug, then slapped my father on his back and flopped onto the sofa.

Why did she have to come? I couldn't even enjoy my own cousin in my own home without having to put up with his girlfriend—excuse me, *fiancée*. Saturday was not looking good. I had Tameka in my house taking up time with Alonzo, and then I would be spending the rest of the day with Shontessa.

"Good to see you again, Tameka," Daddy said. "Didn't know you were a big football fan."

"I'm not. I'm just dropping Alonzo off because his car is in the shop. I'm headed out to go shopping as soon as I leave here."

Good. She's leaving.

"Oh, why don't you join us? We're going shopping, too," Mom said.

Please say no, Tameka. Please say no.

"Sure. I'll even drive. I just need to stop at Happy Hardware first. Then I'll take you wherever you want to go."

"That would be great! Especially since my car has been making some funny noises lately," Mom said.

"I keep telling you to get it fixed!" Daddy yelled from the sofa. "Instead of going to the mall, you need to go see the mechanic."

Mom shrugged and ignored him and rushed us out of the house. Me, Mom, Shontessa, and Tameka all piled into Tameka's huge blue SUV.

"Cool car!" Shontessa said. "It's so nice and roomy!"

"I can't deal with a small car; it makes me feel cramped," Tameka said. "My last car was a hatchback, and every time I got into it, I felt like I was trying to fold a ladder into a coffee cup."

I wasn't impressed by her big car. I said, "Yeah, but it's almost too big. I bet when you get a parking ticket downtown, you get another one in the suburbs at the same time."

Tameka laughed, and we all headed out to the Happy Hardware store. Happy Hardware was an enormous store that looked more like a warehouse. It sold planks of lumber, nails and hammers, seeds in small envelopes, and tall plants in fat flowerpots. It smelled like appliances and paint and wood and tools. Shontessa and I peeled off from Mom and Tameka and began exploring the store, not that I thought there was anything for me at Happy Hardware. Normally, there was not a single thing a fifth-grade girl would want to buy at a hardware store. But while wandering down an aisle, I saw clotheslines. I picked one up and headed to the checkout.

"What do you want with that?" Shontessa asked.

"This is what we could use to jump Double Dutch!" I said.

"You should save your money for when we get to the mall," she said.

"It's my Christmas money and I can spend it on whatever I want. I want a Double Dutch rope."

"Did I hear someone say Double Dutch?" Tameka was coming up behind us in line.

"Yeah, my mother has been promising to teach me Double Dutch," I explained to Tameka, not that it was any of her business. "We're going to use this clothesline for a rope."

"I know how to jump Double Dutch," said Tameka. "I used to do it all the time when I was a kid. I never see kids jumping rope nowadays."

"Me and Shontessa saw some girls jumping on YouTube. I want to be like them."

"I've gotten way better since Thanksgiving," said Shontessa. "I bet I can outjump you."

"What makes you think that? And where did you get the chance to jump?" I knew Shontessa had to be telling another of her tall tales.

"I've been thinking about it a lot," Shontessa said. "I'm going to get a designer jump rope and a Double Dutch outfit to jump in at one of the after-Christmas sales."

"A Double Dutch outfit? What is that?" Now my mother had joined us.

"Oh, it looks like a cheerleader's uniform," Shontessa said. "Only cuter."

"I never heard of that," said my mother. "All I ever needed was a pair of tennis shoes and I was good to go. Speaking of good to go, you all ready to go to the mall?"

"I have an idea," said Tameka as we walked out to the parking lot.

We went outside to the Happy Hardware parking lot. It was a sunny Saturday with a serious nip in the air. Just enough chill to make sure you didn't dawdle as you walked back to the car. It seemed like, on bright winter days, the cold air made everything sharper and clearer, like a high-definition TV picture.

"Let's jump rope," said Tameka.

"Girl, you're crazy," Mom said. But I could see there was a part of her that wanted to do it. She was watching Tameka with big excitement in her eyes and she followed right behind her.

"Let's go over here where there are no cars." Tameka reached out for me to hand her the clothesline. "I haven't jumped in so long, I probably can't do anything. But it would be fun to try."

"And maybe I can shake off some of the calories from

Christmas dinner," said Mom.

"It's kind of cold out here," Shontessa said, and I shivered in agreement.

"You'll warm up once you start moving," Mom said as she unwound the clothesline. Wow, was she actually going to do it? Would I finally get to see my mother, the Double Dutcher?

"Jayla, take the other end," Mom said. "Let's get Shontessa in the rope first, so we can put a little heat on her bones."

"I'm cold, too! Why can't I jump first?"

"Don't worry. Turning the rope will generate plenty of heat, too," Mom said. "Turning is as much exercise as jumping and requires as much skill."

Shontessa jumped in as soon as we started turning. She jumped in a kind of raggedy way a few times before she missed.

"Can I get another go, Aunt Sherry?" she asked immediately.

"Okay, one more. Then it's Jayla's turn."

This time she lasted longer. I think because on her second go, we all sang a jump-rope chant. Tameka started us off.

"Miss Lucy had a baby. She named him Tiny Tim. She put him in the bathtub to see if he could swim…"

Tameka was smiling at Shontessa as she chanted. Shontessa was soaking up all the attention like a shriveled sponge in dirty dishwater.

"He ate up all the water. He ate up all the soap. He tried to eat the bathtub, but it wouldn't go down his throat."

When was her turn ever going to end? Tameka had better turn and chant just as much for me when I got a go.

When we got to the part about *In came the doctor. In came the nurse. In came the lady with the alligator purse*, Shontessa said, "I'm getting an alligator purse for my birthday."

Why anyone would want a purse that looks like an alligator or made from an alligator's scaly, scratchy skin was beyond me. If I were to get a new purse, I'd want it to be made from...maybe cookies? Or my favorite snack, Krazy Krunchies. Yeah, that would be cool. I could break off a piece of my purse whenever I got hungry.

"It's my turn now, Miss Alligator," I said when Shontessa finally missed. I thrust the rope out to her.

"I am *not* an alligator. I said I have an alligator *purse*. You're so dumb," she said.

"You did *not* say you have an alligator purse. You said you were going to get one for your birthday, but you probably won't."

"Are you calling me a liar?"

"Girls!" Mom warned us and gave each of us a look. She should've only looked at Shontessa because I hadn't done anything wrong. But I stuck my tongue out at her back and muttered, "See you later, alligator," at Shontessa under my breath, low enough so only she could hear it.

Evidently, Tameka heard it, too.

"Come on, Jayla," Tameka whispered to me. "Don't act like a baby." Then a little louder she said, "Your time to shine." She took Shontessa's end, so it was her and Mom turning. Immediately, I could see the difference. The ropes became fluid hoops whipping over and out in perfect curves.

"Ready to learn how to jump Double Dutch?" Mom asked.

She didn't have to ask me twice. I ran over to the ropes and then hesitated. Mom and Tameka had a beat going: *thwop, swoop, thwop, swoop*. How could I ever manage to dive into that river of rope?

You know how in old movies, a man will swing a watch on a chain and then the person watching will fall into a trance? That's how I felt watching the ropes.

I jumped in, but I missed.

"Aim for the middle of the rope. Don't be shy; go for it strong," Mom said.

I stood at the edge of the rope. Mom was facing me, smiling. Shontessa was standing across from me, her arms folded against her chest like she was hiding stolen jewels under her coat. She was probably hoping I'd miss again. I could almost feel her sending poison-coated thoughts in my direction.

"Stop turning for a minute, Sherry," Tameka said. "Have Jayla stand in the middle." She pointed and I moved to where she directed me. "Now, when I say go, you jump like this."

Tameka demonstrated a jump that was not too high, feet together, steady rhythm. I jumped along with her, getting into the same step and time. It wasn't fast and fancy like the YouTube girls. I wondered if she was trying to make me look dull and dowdy like her. But I went ahead and imitated her exactly.

"Okay, now you're going to do the very same thing while we turn. Don't start till we say *go*," she said.

If she said *go*, I didn't hear it. I was standing in the rope, waiting to start, and next thing I knew, the rope was hitting my leg.

"Jump when we yell go, Jayla!" Mom said. "Focus!"

So I focused my mind and tuned my ears to hear *go*. I thought I heard it and started jumping as hard as I could. Mom was staring at me. "Jayla, nobody said *go*. We haven't started turning. Settle down and wait for the cue."

The next time, I timed it right. Both Mom and Tameka yelled "Go!" and I went. I jumped up and down, not too high, feet together, steady rhythm. The ropes swung over my head and under my feet and all I felt was joy. Even once I missed, I still felt warm and wonderful on the inside because I was proud of what I had just done, and tingly and bouncy on the outside because the sun was bright and the air was nippy and it made everything exciting.

"You go, girl!" Mom shouted and gave me a high five.

I raised my hand to get a high five from Shontessa, too. She slapped my hand and she gave a smirk to go with it. But that was OK with me. I was jumping Double Dutch. And I knew I was good.

Tameka dropped her end and ran over to give me a high five, but I put the rope back into her hand and said, "Keep turning. I want to go again."

Shontessa talked over me and said, "Miss Tameka, are you going to jump?"

"Girl, you know it!"

Tameka handed me her end and stood at an angle, but once Mom and I started turning, she didn't jump in—it was like she *flowed* into the rope. She did a pop up, turned around, did another pop up, crisscrossed her feet, turned around several more times, then kept on jumping for what seemed like a long, long time.

"Wow, Miss Tameka!" squealed Shontessa. "That was fantastic. Wasn't it, Jayla?"

"Yeah, she was okay." I said. "Mom, let's see you."

Tameka and I began turning. "I'm coming in by Tameka's door," she said. *Door? What door?* And then I realized that she meant she would be jumping into the rope from Tameka's side. I can't really say she "entered the door"—she flew in.

"Skin the rope!" she yelled. What did *that* mean? But I

felt Tameka's side of the rope increase in speed, so I moved my arms as rapidly as I could to keep up with Mom's feet. "Faster!" she yelled again, and Tameka and I made the ropes move so fast that I could hardly see them.

Mom turned around, then turned around again. She leaped in the air to do a pop up, then she was back in the rope jumping faster than an Olympic sprinter headed for the finish line.

All of a sudden, it was like my middle-aged mother disappeared and a teenage jump-rope ninja took over her body. Her hat began to slip from her head, so she snatched it off and threw it away. She unbuttoned her coat and managed to shuck it off without missing a step.

Free of the heavy coat, she did an extra high pop up, and then she did what the cheerleaders called a C jump. That's when you jump and curve your body backward, so that it's in the shape of the letter *C*. Then she was back to jumping hard. Her breath puffed out of her like the trail of a jet plane crossing the sky. After what felt like hours, she missed. She huffed and puffed and leaned against Tameka, winded but grinning.

"I haven't jumped in years!" Mom said once she caught her breath. "But that was so much fun!"

"Can I get a go?"

I looked around and realized a group of two or three people had been watching us. The person who spoke was a woman older than my mother. I couldn't imagine someone that old jumping Double Dutch. Plus, she was heavy. She didn't just have a little pouch around the waist or a little padding on the butt. She was a Big Girl.

"Come on in!" shouted Tameka. She and Mom started turning again.

Big Girl jumped in. And to my surprise, she could move! She started off a little wobbly, but it wasn't long before she was into a rhythm, and I could tell she knew what she was doing. "Look at me! Look at me!" she kept shouting while laughing. "Look at me—doing Double Dutch after all these years!"

When she finished, there were high fives all around. And next thing we knew, someone else was asking, "Can I get a turn?" Mom and Tameka began turning again, and pretty soon there was a line of people in the Happy Hardware parking lot waiting to get a go. We ended up taking turns turning rope for another hour and a half.

I finally got to see my mom jump Double Dutch. It was almost like I didn't recognize her as the same lady who bought groceries and braided hair and ate too much at Thanksgiving and Christmas. We never made it to the mall. I guessed Daddy would be happy that we ran out of time to shop. But the $6.50 of my Christmas money that I spent on the clothesline made my Saturday a very well-spent Saturday. Even if I did have to spend it with Shontessa. And Tameka.

CHAPTER 6

The way Shontessa acts now, it's hard to believe we were ever friends. When we were little, her mother would often drop her off at my house or vice versa, and we'd play. A lot of times, the grown-ups would hire a babysitter to watch the both of us while they went out somewhere. We'd play Roblox together, or watch TV, or play with dolls.

But everything changed when Shontessa turned thirteen. Suddenly, she thought everything about me was babyish. If I wanted to make something with Legos, she would just sit and watch but not help build anything. When I brought out my LOL dolls, she refused to play with them even though she used to love collecting them, just like I did.

Shontessa always acted like she thought she was cute, but I never let it bother me. She did look good in her clothes, and she always managed to get her mother to buy her the latest styles. Me, I had to beg my mother to buy me anything. She was an accountant and her favorite word was *budget*. As in, "New sneakers? That's not in the budget," or "You want me to buy what? I don't think we can squeeze that into the budget." It felt like I'd been begging her for years to buy me a phone, but she never budged on that.

It's too bad you can't order friends online and have a brand-new playmate delivered to your door. I so wished I had someone to play with, to talk to. I wasn't really close to any of the kids at school and hadn't been since Maya left. Maya and I had been BFFs since first grade. We used to pretend we were sisters, in part because people said we looked alike—we both wore braids—and in part because neither one of us had real sisters. Maya wasn't an only child; she had two brothers. Once when she invited me to go with her family to Six Flags, a lady saw all of us together and told Mr. and Mrs. Oliver, "What a perfect family! Two parents, two boys, and two girls!" We didn't correct her, just smiled and said thank you.

Because me and Maya always hung together, I never really got tight with the other girls in my class. Between her and Shontessa, I always had someone to hang with. But Maya left at the end of fourth grade last year, and the nice version of Shontessa had already split, and so far this school year I hadn't really connected with anyone else. Everybody already had best friends picked out. It's not like anybody was mean to me or anything like that. Nobody boxed me out. But nobody brought me in either.

Like one time, the teacher divided us up into groups of three. We had a story to read and questions to go with it. Me, Jade, and Kierra were supposed to discuss the questions together. But Jade and Kierra basically talked to one another and never paid me any attention.

"What's the difference between *immigrate* with an *i* and *emigrate* with an *e*?" asked Kierra, pointing to the two different places the word showed up in the passage.

"I think I know," I started, but Jade cut me off.

"We'd better check the glossary," Jade said and turned to the back of the book. She found the word pretty quickly and read it out loud.

"*Emigrate* with an *e* means to leave one country and go to another."

"I thought the other *immigrate* meant that," Kierra said to Jade.

"It's almost the same, but it's the other way around," I tried to explain.

They looked puzzled so Jade said, "We'd better look that one up, too." And when she found it she read, "Immigrate: to come to a new country or place."

They both still looked like they didn't understand, but instead of letting me try to explain it again, they asked Mr. Kurata to tell them what the difference was. I should have asked the teacher for a definition, too. What is the word for someone who finds themselves stuck in a new place even though they haven't left home?

That's why I was looking forward to another Niece Night. I was disappointed that time when Alonzo didn't really hang out with me because of that phone call. I'm sure it was Tameka on the phone, interfering with our Niece Night time. I guess Cousin Julia had a point about cell phones causing trouble.

But I was sure this time would be better. Me and Cousin Alonzo had plans to hang out. This particular Niece Night was just me and him on the afternoon before New Year's Eve and he said that we'd be making some New Year's Eve food.

Alonzo could cook. In addition to a slammin' macaroni and cheese, he could do fried chicken real well and potato salad and most anything Daddy called "fat-belly" food. He had started teaching me how to fix different dishes. I wondered what we'd be cooking.

"Alonzo, why don't you teach me how to cook candy?" He was wiping off the kitchen counter and stopped to turn and look at me and laugh.

"Cook candy? Now that's a first. I don't believe I've ever even seen a recipe for candy." He smoothed out a wrinkled piece of notebook paper that had the recipe for what he wanted to fix today.

"So what are we cooking?"

"How about some black-eyed peas, but instead of with ham hocks, we're going to do it with turkey." I saw where he had a bag of the peas soaking on the counter. He was cooking a big batch of peas and collards, plus some cornbread that he was sending home with me for my family.

"More turkey! Didn't we have enough of that at Thanksgiving?" I remembered Alonzo's black-eyed peas from last year's New Year's Day. He said eating black-eyed peas at the start of the New Year brings you luck. I didn't want him to tamper with that recipe. It was good.

"I'm fixing it so that it's a healthier dish, Jayla-Jayla. Tryin' to cut down on the salt."

"What's wrong with salt? Salt makes food taste good."

"Salt's bad for your blood. I'm trying to keep my pressure down."

"Who's pressing you, Tameka?" I knew it. He didn't really want to get married. She was pressing him into it.

"No, that's not what I mean. You know, high blood pressure."

"What's that?"

"It's a disease some people get, especially if they don't exercise or eat right. But you don't have to worry about that, like your mother does. I'm going to teach you how to cook lots of veggies and how to season them up good without a lot of salt."

"What do you mean 'I don't have to worry about that like my mother'?"

Alonzo looked like someone who got called on in class but didn't know the right answer.

"Didn't mean nothing. Let's just fix these black-eyed peas. Fill that pot with water, put a bay leaf in it, and set it on the burner." I did what he told me to do, then I turned on the heat.

"Does my mother have pressure?"

Alonzo's phone rang, so he didn't say anything back to me. He turned slightly and answered the phone with an enthusiastic "Hey, baby!"

I didn't have to see the screen to know who he was talking to.

"The wedding's not for six months. Do we have to decide that now?" As he talked, he gestured for me to open the box of cornbread mix. "Okay, text me the choices and I'll let you know what I think," he said into the phone and then hung up.

"What all do you have to do to get ready for the wedding?" I asked.

"Tameka's got me running all over the place with first one thing, then another."

"Running all over the place—aren't you having the wedding at the church?"

"We are, but you have to do a lot of stuff in advance: reserve the space, hire a caterer, plan the reception, and a bunch of other things. You can't just show up with a bunch of your friends and family and say, 'Let's party!'"

"But that's pretty much how we do Niece Night."

"Well, Wife Night is a little more complicated than that."

It seemed like everything with family was always complicated. We were quiet for a minute while I stirred the batter for the cornbread and he scrolled through his phone reading texts from Tameka. He smiled at something he was reading. *Hmph...* She got smiles and as soon as she asked him to do something, he jumped to it. I asked him a simple question about my mother and her high blood pressure, but he refused to answer me.

"Alonzo, is my mother real sick?"

"Girl, stop worrying," he said, but he didn't look at me when he said it. I was about to ask him again when he said, "Turn down the heat on the peas; they're boiling a bit too fast."

I did as he asked, but then I said, "Just exactly what does high blood pressure do to you?"

"Don't worry about it. Let's just fix these peas, Jayla-Jayla." He picked up a spice jar and flourished it. "You know what's the best thing to put in your black-eyed peas?"

"No, what?" I looked at the label on the jar. "Thyme?"

"No. The best thing to put in a dish is your teeth!"

I couldn't argue with that.

CHAPTER 7

When I become boss of the world, I'm going to make the month of January against the law. I hate being cold. I hate snow and ice. Woolen sweaters make me itch, and heavy boots make my legs feel like they're locked up in jail. I don't even like it when the weather is so bad they cancel school. At least at school you're with other kids. At home, you're stuck inside the house with nothing to do, especially if you're an only child.

It was a gray and ugly and shivery Wednesday, and the air smelled like there was a chance of freezing rain. But I was in a sunny mood. That day, I was going to get Ms. Cooper to allow me to have a Double Dutch team.

The first day after the holiday break was Monday, and I had gone to see Mrs. Sanchez, my classroom teacher, to ask her if I could start a Double Dutch team. Mrs. Sanchez told me that was something the principal would have to approve. The principal, Mr. Washington, had about ten people waiting to see him that first day. So I went to see him Tuesday morning. He said, "If the gym teacher wants to do it, fine." So I went to see Ms. Cooper. I didn't have PE on Tuesdays, so I had to go by the gym during my lunch period on Wednesday. You could feel the energy of a crowd of children cheering, and the gym smelled like sneakers and sweat. I couldn't decide if this was a good smell or a bad one. Ms. Cooper was stacking mats in the closet when I walked up to her.

"Ms. Cooper, can you help me with something?"

"Depends. What do you want?" She closed the closet door, crossed her arms, and looked down her nose at me.

"I'd like for us to have a Double Dutch team here at Taylor Elementary School."

"Double Dutch? You know how to jump?"

"Yes." Well, I'd only had one lesson, but that counted.

"And you know enough girls who want to jump?"

"Yes." I didn't, but I was pretty certain I could round up some people. Maybe some boys, too.

"And who would coach the team?"

"Well, Mrs. Sanchez told me to ask Mr. Washington and Mr. Washington told me you could do it."

"Like I don't already have enough to do." She grabbed

hold of a long pole and went over to one of the high, narrow windows. She used the hook at the end of the pole to crack the window and let in some much-needed air.

"Oh, Ms. Cooper, it wouldn't be a lot of work. It'll be easy; it really will!" I gave her my sweetest little-kid smile, the one that always works on Daddy when I ask him to buy me some ice cream.

"When is this 'easy' program supposed to take place?"

"Couldn't we do it after school?"

"Maybe the after-school coordinator will do it; ask Ms. McMillan."

Oh no, not Ms. McMillan. She was the most clueless woman known to man. She was the grown-up version of my cousin Antwon. When she was in charge, nothing ever got done. At least not done right. The kids in her after-school group got stuck doing dumb stuff like sitting in a room listening to the all-news station on the radio. Or she made them make crafts using toilet paper tubes.

"Ms. Cooper, can't *you* do the after-school program? Please? We'll be really good, we really will!"

"I don't have any time during the instructional day, and I can't stay after to start a new program. Ms. McMillan is the only one who could do it." Ms. Cooper left the room and left me standing in the big, empty gym feeling big and empty myself.

Ms. McMillan didn't have a classroom or an office. She didn't even have a desk, and she was so dizzy that I'm not sure she even knew she was supposed to have any of the stuff that most grown-ups expect. Ms. McMillan reminded me of a giraffe—tall, skinny, and with what probably would have been a graceful neck, but she tended to hunch. She wore her hair in two huge braids that framed her face like the weave of a basket. She didn't come in until half an hour before school let out, and she sat with her tablet in an alcove near the gym. She piled her belongings on a folding chair next to the folding chair she slouched in.

The chair beside her was stacked with a jillion things: a book titled *101 Recreational Activities for Kids*, an empty fried chicken bucket, a tennis ball wedged between the seat and the seat back, a volleyball under the seat, and a plastic rope draped over the seat back.

"Is that a jump rope?" I asked, pointing.

"Yes, yes it is. I'm going to be starting a new jump rope group."

I wasn't sure I heard her right. "A jump rope group?" I repeated like a dummy.

"Yes, yes. For the second semester, I'm going to try to put together a jump rope activity. Not a lot of kids these days know how to jump rope. You want to be in the class?"

Ms. McMillan was already starting a jump rope club?

That would be perfect!

"Yeah! I want to jump rope—that's why I came to see you, actually. Can it be a Double Dutch team?"

"Oh. I only know single." She looked a bit distressed, like I was making things too complicated for her. "People who do Double Dutch do a lot of tricks. Do you know any tricks?"

"I can do tricks!" I said. I'd never done any tricks in the rope, but I was sure I could learn some, especially since Mom knew how. If I had inherited her nose and her hair, certainly I had her feet and her moves.

"Very, very good. We'll start next week."

So I figured I was wrong. Silly Ms. McMillan was going to make something work after all.

But I later found out I was wrong about being wrong.

———

We were supposed to have started the Double Dutch group the second week in January, but Ms. McMillan couldn't seem to get anything together. So by the time she had a group of seven kids, January was over, and it was the second week of February.

"Okay, okay. Who knows how to turn?" Ms. McMillan asked as she stared at the semicircle of five girls and two boys staring back at her. I raised my hand and Terrie, a girl I knew from science club, raised her hand.

"Good, good. The two of you grab the ends," Ms. McMillan said and waved toward the rope laid out on the gym floor. "Let's get started. Line up, line up! Davon, you can start." I shouldn't have raised my hand—I wanted to be the first to jump! But I went ahead and picked up the rope.

Davon sprinted to the front of the line. He had on black high-top sneakers and a black T-shirt. He was bouncing around like he had Angry Birds inside of him. Davon jumped in. He had a heavy step like he was breaking boulders beneath his feet. But he could go. He was good. When he missed, it was Nia's go. She stood there, staring as we turned. And turned. And turned.

When is she going to jump in? I was thinking. My arms were wearing out. Then it hit me. *This is her first time.*

"Stop for a minute," I said to Terrie and then to Nia, "Why don't you stand in the middle of the rope?"

Nia looked like I had saved her life and stepped in between the two collapsed ropes that laid side by side on the floor.

"When we start turning, just hop up and down like a bunny rabbit."

Nia looked uncertain, but not as petrified as she had when standing by the side with the two ropes whipping back and forth. She looked at me, I looked at her, then me and Terrie looked at each other and started turning. And Nia started jumping. Up and down. Up and down. Nia started grinning. She was doing it! Up and down, doing Double Dutch.

"I think we've got something here. We've got something here!" said Ms. McMillan as she watched Nia grinning and jumping.

A girl named Taylor and a boy named Kim went next and then—*finally*—Ms. McMillan let me and Terrie stop turning and get a go. Taylor and Nia switched places with us, and their turning was so sloppy I almost wanted to cry. How could I ever hope to get a decent turn when the ropes sloped off to the side like drool dripping down a baby's chin? When Terrie and me turned, it had started off the beat at first, but it didn't take long before we had the ropes making a steady sway. And when I saw my mother and Tameka turning, their rope hadn't just done a steady sway; it was a swinging beat. Their turning inspired you to jump.

But these two? Their rope-turning reminded me of spaghetti sliding off a spoon. I looked to Ms. McMillan, certain she could see the problem. She looked at me and said, "Are you scared to jump in, Jayla?"

Scared? Didn't she see the loose and lopsided way the ropes were going? I wanted to fuss, but I didn't. I just said, "Ms. McMillan, could you turn for me, please?"

It was only then that she moved her attention to the turners and realized what was the matter.

"Davon, Davon, you and I are going to turn for Jayla."

Davon had strength and speed. Ms. McMillan had height and length. Together they made the rope swing and sing. I jumped in, and my heart was beating as fast as my feet.

"Go, Jayla! Go, Jayla! Go, Jayla!" I heard them chanting. I felt like my heart would burst out of my chest. I wished Mom and Cousin Julia could see me. They'd be so proud, and they'd know I could be just as good as them. I wished Shontessa could see me, too. She'd be jealous. She'd be mad 'cause I was better than her. She would see how I could show her up.

And that's when I missed.

But I didn't care 'cause I had jumped longer than anybody else, even Davon. And we finally had a team.

CHAPTER 8

Double Dutch practice took place once a week, on Tuesdays after school. We met in a corner of the gym. The middle of the gym was occupied by the volleyball team.

"You coming to Double Dutch tomorrow, Terrie?" I fell into step with her as we walked into the school building on Monday morning. The February air was crisp and cold, a sharp contrast to the comforting warmth inside the school.

"Yeah, I guess," she said. "Although I can't turn as good as you."

"You'll get better," I told her. "Plus, you jump real well."

"You think so?" She shifted her backpack, and I helped adjust the shoulder strap that had slipped down her arm.

"Yeah! You're great! Come back so we can all keep getting better. Have you seen Double Dutch on YouTube?"

She hadn't but said she'd take a look. By this time, we were well into the building and headed to classrooms in different directions. I skipped down the hallway to my class, thinking about tomorrow's practice.

When me, Jade, and Kierra were grouped together for the social studies lesson, I thought about inviting them to jump rope. But I heard them talking about a music program they were going to tomorrow, so I figured they'd say no. In the cafeteria, I saw Nia sitting at the end of a long table where everyone was chatting and laughing except for her. The smell of chocolate milk and chicken tenders surrounded me as I slipped in the seat beside her.

"Double Dutch is tomorrow. Are you gonna be there?"

She took a long swallow of apple juice before she answered. "I don't know," she said.

"I hope you come back. You'll have a good time. I promise!"

Nia said okay, but I wasn't entirely convinced.

"You comin' to Double Dutch tomorrow, Davon?" By the time I ran into Davon, it was dismissal time. He was jogging across the playground.

"I'll be there," he said, then he went into a rap. "I'll be there jumping and jammin'. Bangin' the floor with my feet like an athlete with a beat."

I laughed as he broke into a run to meet up with his ride home.

The chants were one of the best things about jumping rope, after the actual jumping. Of course, I had gotten my mother to tell me some of the ones she used to do when she was a kid, like this one:

Cinderella, dressed in yella,
Went upstairs to kiss her fella.
Made a mistake
And kissed a snake.
How many doctors
Did it take?
1, 2, 3, 4, 5...

Then you'd keep counting to see how high you could go. The one I liked best was Charlie Chaplin. It went like this:

Charlie Chaplin went to France
To teach the girls the hula-hula dance.
A heel, a toe, around we go.
Salute to the captain, curtsy to the queen.
Touch the bottom of the submarine.
I wish I had a nickel, I wish I had a dime.
I wish I had a sweetheart to love me all the time.
I'd make him wash the dishes. I'd make him scrub the floor.
And when he got finished, I'd kick him out the door.

I liked that one because Mom said you would act out the statements in the chant—take a bow to curtsy to the queen, bend down and touch the ground at the part where you touch the bottom of the submarine, pretend to wash dishes, all while jumping. I wanted to try to see if I could make all the moves without missing. I was going to ask Ms. McMillan if we could do that at practice tomorrow.

All day Monday, I had reminded anybody who had come before to come back, and I invited some additional people to try it, too. I was looking forward to a bunch of people at practice.

But on Tuesday, when I got to the gymnasium, nobody was there except Ms. McMillan and Nia. Even the volleyball team was absent.

"Where is everybody?"

"I think they went to the hip-hop program," Nia said. "That's where Davon said he was going."

Turns out, there was a special after-school workshop on rap music. It figured Davon would be there, since he already thought he was a rapper. Everybody was probably there. And here I was with only Nia. Because that wasn't enough people, Ms. McMillan dismissed us.

But I didn't let it bother me. The hip-hop program was a special one-time thing. Next week, there wouldn't be any conflict. Next week would be better.

But every time next week came, something went wrong. School closed for a snow day. The gymnasium floor was being cleaned and polished. Folks forgot to show up. By March, seven kids had dropped down to four: me, Davon, Terrie, and, surprisingly, Nia. Except for Nia, we had gotten better week by week. Nia was kind of clunky, but she kept coming back. Terrie was a pretty steady jumper; she could last a long time in the rope. Davon could do pop ups; that's when someone can jump up high, then come back down into the rope on time and in step. I could do pop ups, too but mine weren't as impressive as Davon's. I was still looking for a stunt I could do in the rope that would make me stand out.

Ms. McMillan had jumped rope as a girl, but it was single rope only, so she didn't know any good Double Dutch tricks. She kept forgetting to bring her tablet or even a cell phone, so we could show her some YouTube videos to get ideas. I wished Mom would buy me my own phone! Eleven was old enough. Shontessa got her own phone four years ago, when she was ten. At least that's what she claimed.

"Mom?" I said one Tuesday night after practice. "When are you going to jump Double Dutch again?"

"You still harping on that?" Mom was chopping up a red bell pepper for a salad.

"I need to learn some tricks. None of the people on the team know how to do anything cool."

"Could you hand me the onion? Or better yet, why don't you help me by cutting it?"

I opened the refrigerator but didn't see any onions. I looked in the vegetable bin on the kitchen counter, but I didn't see any onions. "Where are the onions?"

Mom stopped, holding her knife midair. "No onions? Oh well, I suppose we can have a salad without onions. Although without onions, the salad tastes about as boring as waiting for your phone to charge."

"If I had my own phone, I'd never complain about it being boring while it charged up," I said, trying to drop a hint.

"Forget it, Jayla. You're still too young." I was about to explain that eleven was not too young to have a cell phone, but she cut me off.

"If you want to prove how grown-up you are, help me with dinner. Put the lettuce in that bowl over there"—she gestured with the knife—"and get the tomatoes out of the—" She stopped as she looked at the tomato keeper and saw there were no tomatoes there. "Oh. Our salad won't have any tomatoes, either. I didn't realize we'd eaten the last one."

"And there won't be any lettuce in the salad, either. I don't see any in the refrigerator." I held the door wide open, so she could lean in and look. She sighed and looked at her watch.

"Your father won't be home for another half hour or so. I guess we have enough time to run to the store and buy some salad fixings. Can't have a salad without lettuce. Or tomatoes. Or onions."

Ten minutes later, we were in the grocery store. I was pushing the cart up and down the aisles. In my head, I was pretending to drive. I pushed the cart fast, moving way ahead. Mom had to trot to keep up with me. We had left the produce section, and I was steering us down the aisle with the cookies and crackers.

"Mom, can we get some Krazy Krunchies?" Krazy Krunchies look like potato chips but are sweet like cookies and they taste sort of like popcorn and candy all at the same time. I picked up the king-size bag and put it in the shopping cart.

"No, we're not buying that," Mom said. But I didn't take the chips out the basket and she didn't either.

"They're so-o-o YFYT. Don't you like them too?" I said.

"What is YF...what?"

"YFYT. Yummy for your tummy."

"I wouldn't mind having something to snack on, but..." She didn't finish her sentence because a voice rang out from way down the aisle.

"Sherry, how you doing?" *Good.* Maybe whoever it was would distract her and she'd leave the Krazy Krunchies in the cart.

It was Uncle Mike and Antwon. "Hi, Antwon," I said.

"Hi, Jayla. What are you all doing here?" said Antwon.

Buying groceries, duh—what else would someone be doing at a grocery store?

"We ran out of lettuce," my mother explained, "and I decided I need that and a few other things to finish making dinner."

"Krazy Krunchies for dinner? YFYT!" Antwon said, picking up the bag and tossing it in the air like a ball. Well, he was right about at least one thing.

"Really, Sherry?" Uncle Mike said in a voice that sounded like a principal who was about to hand out a punishment. "You're not buying that invitation to heart disease, are you? Didn't I hear you at Thanksgiving saying you had high blood pressure?"

"Yeah, Mike. I'm trying to eat right—that's why I'm here buying salad fixings." She gestured at the lettuce and tomatoes and onions in the cart.

"I don't like that kind of food," said Antwon. "That stuff grows out of the ground; it has dirt on it."

"Well, don't undo all your good work eating that Krazy Krunchies crap," Uncle Mike said. "It's nothing but sugar coated with salt and grease."

"Sugar, salt, and grease make food taste good!" said Antwon.

"They sure do," Mom said, surprising me by agreeing with Antwon. "And you can't stop eating them once you get started. I can eat a whole bag this size all by myself!"

I agreed with Antwon, too. "See! I told you Krazy Krunchies are good!" I said, putting an extra bag into the basket. "You can have a bag to yourself and me and Daddy can eat this one."

"So you're going to poison your whole family into high blood pressure using Krazy Krunchies?" Uncle Mike said to Mom.

"Krazy Krunchies aren't poison," I said.

"That's right!" said Antwon. "Krazy Krunchies are salty, sugary, greasy fun!"

"Well, it's not good for someone with hypertension," Uncle Mike said.

There was that word again. What exactly was hypertension? *Hyper*—that's when someone gets real excited. *Tension*—that's when you feel tight and nervous. Was Mom nervous about something?

I looked up at her and she turned her face away. Then she took the bags of Krazy Krunchies and put them back on the shelf. Uncle Mike didn't buy Antwon any Krazy Krunchies, either. Antwon had finally said something I liked, but then the grown-ups threw up a stop sign on what we wanted, and Antwon snapped back to his regular self. As they walked away, I heard him ask his father, "How many peas are in a peanut?"

That night, right after I did my word problems but before I got started on conjugating verbs for Señora Pellicato, I googled *hypertension*. Hypertension also goes by the name high blood pressure. The website said over one billion people in the whole wide world are living with hypertension and 9.4 million people die from it. OMG, that's a whole lot of people. Could my mother end up being one of the people who die from hypertension? I also saw that people can make changes to get better, like losing weight, eating healthy, and getting physical exercise. It's too bad grown-ups don't have to take gym at work the way kids do at school.

I guessed Mom thought Krazy Krunchies weren't healthy, so she changed her mind about buying them. But they taste so-o-o good—they can't be that bad, can they? Although Mom is a little big and kinda round, Daddy always said to her, "You're not fat; you're PHAT—you've got Pretty Hips And Thighs!" My mom *is* pretty, just not with that music-video body she had when she was young. Back then, she used to get lots of exercise, she told me. But as she got older, she let it slide.

Even once I had finished all my homework and laid down in bed, I was still thinking about high blood pressure. If Mom had it, did that mean I would catch it, too? And what could I do about it?

CHAPTER 9

Sometimes I think it would be fun to have other kids in the house, although if I had a brother as empty-headed as Antwon, I'd get exhausted trying to correct all of his mistakes. Or, good grief, if I had a sister like Shontessa! OMG. She thought that because she was in the eighth grade and I was only in the fifth grade that made her smarter than me. That didn't mean anything. It just meant she had three more years' experience at being awful. I could not stand her constant bragging about all her electronic gadgets or her designer clothes or fancy phone. Like back at Christmastime when we were jumping rope at the hardware store parking lot. Okay, I admit it. She was good. A couple of people had come up to her and told her things like "Work it, girl!" or "If you could bottle up all that energy and sell it, you'd make a million."

Shontessa soaked up all that praise the way a scratchy scalp soaks up hair grease. "Jayla, I could probably get my own reality show," she said, tossing her long, fake hair all over the place like she was already one of the Real Housewives of Double Dutch.

"Yeah, yeah," I said. "Next time you buy a weave, get one with a brain attached to it."

That's why I liked Cousin Alonzo so much. He didn't come with teenage drama. It had been more than a month since I last saw Alonzo, on Niece Night just before the year ended. And the time before that, when he and Tameka had come over Saturday after Christmas, I didn't get to talk to him much because he watched the football game with my father and I had been jumping Double Dutch in the Happy Hardware parking lot. That had been fun even though I'd had to put up with Tameka. Anyway, now it was the last Saturday of February and I was about to see him for the first time since the holidays.

I was real glad when Cousin Alonzo had called and suggested that since it was Black History Month, it would be a good time to go downtown to the Smithsonian's National Museum of African American History and Culture. Daddy was taking me, and Alonzo was going to meet up with us there for a program they were having on African dance and drumming.

When Daddy said we were going to walk to the train station, at first I was disappointed. The temperature called for a jacket, boots, two sweaters, and three scarves, plus I had lost my gloves, so I'd have to keep my hands stuffed in my pockets. I can't say I liked the frigid air, but it made me walk fast and the fast walking made me feel peppy. I liked that I could almost keep pace with Daddy. I considered that proof that I was growing up. Pretty soon, they'd have to stop treating me like a kid. Pretty soon, they'd have to let me have a phone and a bigger allowance.

It was a clear day, but by the time we got on the Metro, a few flakes of snow had started to fall. We boarded the train aboveground, and as I looked out the window, I watched the snow swirling. The snowflakes surrounded the train, blowing all about the window as we sped forward. It made me feel like I was in one of those glass globes where, when you shake it up, little pieces of confetti whirl around. It made me feel cozy even though it was cold. It's weird how a day can feel both heartwarming and bone-chilling at the same time.

Daddy and I got good seats near the front of the museum auditorium. I saved a seat for Alonzo beside me. But when I looked across the aisle, I saw Alonzo was already there. With Tameka. He waved us over—he had saved two seats.

"Let's go join them," Daddy said. He and Alonzo greeted each other with a hand slap.

Tameka looked at me and said, "How're you doing?"

"Fine."

"How's school?"

"Fine." Would she quit with all the nosy questions?

Fortunately, the music started, and stopped her from talking. I was sitting on one side of Tameka, Alonzo on her other side. I leaned over to talk to Alonzo. I figured I could ask some questions of my own, like about the girl Alonzo used to like.

"Alonzo, how's Aisha?"

"Aisha? I don't know no Aisha."

"Who's Aisha?" asked Tameka.

"One of Jayla's little friends, I suppose," Alonzo muttered and turned to look at my father. "It's some kind of cold, ain't it?"

"February is always brutal," said Daddy.

"Aisha knew how to stay warm," I said, jumping back into the conversation. "Don't you remember, Alonzo? She wore a white sweater with fur all around it at Christmas dinner two years ago?"

Alonzo acted like he hadn't heard, and Daddy cut me off before I could repeat myself by saying, "Jayla, that little girl reminds me of you."

I looked at where Daddy was staring and saw a girl in African clothing on the edge of the platform, getting ready to dance. The girl was part of a troupe of four adults, both men and women, and she was the only kid. She wore a royal blue lappa, a piece of African fabric wrapped around her like a skirt, and her hair was in braids. I didn't think she looked like me exactly, but I could tell she was bursting with energy. When the dancers came out, she walked in a way that reminded me of the pride and glory of a peacock combined with the earthiness of a tree.

"She's got stage presence," Tameka said.

"What's stage presence?" I had to ask.

"It's when you perform with your whole self. You take what you're feeling inside and give it to the audience."

"How do you do that?"

"Remember when we were jumping rope at the hardware store and everyone was impressed watching your mother?" said Tameka.

"Yeah! She made everyone else want to jump, too!" I thought back to that day. Once Mom got in the rope, it was like she had set off a magic mojo. It's like how you might not be hungry, not even thinking about food, but when you smell cupcakes baking, the aroma grabs you by the nose and pulls you into the bakery. Everyone coming through the parking lot was drawn over when my mother was jumping. It made them want to be a part of her energy, even if only to watch.

"Your mother has stage presence," Tameka said. "When

she jumped, she gave it her all. She wasn't shy about sharing her soul." Tameka gestured toward the stage, and I noticed her engagement ring. Was she holding out her hand to force me to look at her stupid ring? She continued, "You can tell that girl has both style and—"

"Can I try it on?"

"Try what on?"

"That ring."

"No," said Alonzo. "Engagement rings are for grown women. It's not a toy, Jayla."

"She was waving it my face. I only asked to see it." I could hear my voice rising, but I felt like I couldn't help it.

"*Jayla*," Daddy said and gave me *that look*.

I couldn't believe Alonzo wouldn't let me touch Tameka's stupid ring. All I wanted to do was look at it up close. That's why she was waving it in my face, wasn't it? I couldn't believe how he was acting like she was so special. I didn't see one thing special about Tameka. She didn't dress fancy; today she had on skinny jeans and boots and a turtleneck sweater. Yeah, everything matched, but how much fashion sense did it take to put together a blue top with blue jeans?

What she said about the dancer was interesting, though. I took another look at the girl onstage. She really did have something that made you want to watch her. Although she was the youngest one in the troupe, she definitely danced as hard and as good as the others did. At one point, the drummer came to the front and started playing a solo just for her. Then she really worked it, doing one rhythm with her feet and another with her hands. She smoothly worked her way back, blending her movements into the routine the other dancers were doing. She looked like she was having a fabulous time but was also very serious about the performance. It was an interesting combination of concentrating and celebrating at the same time. Sometimes at church, I would see that same expression on the face of a choir member when she sang the solo. I wondered if I could do the same thing when I jumped Double Dutch.

I went to the ladies' room before we headed home. As I was rinsing my hands, I saw the African dance girl stomp in along with one of the adult dancers.

"I can't believe I messed up my solo!" the girl said with a huff in her voice.

"You were doing a complicated rhythm, Kiki. And you picked right up and got back in step," the older lady said to console her.

"But I messed up!" Kiki snatched off her head wrap and then started retying it. She pulled at it so jerkily that it perched on her head crooked.

"I messed up, too," the lady said.

"When? I didn't see you do anything wrong."

"Remember I was supposed to do that leap when the rhythm changed? I missed my cue."

"Oh…" Kiki said, and I could see her replaying the scene in her mind. "I didn't even notice it when it happened."

"And nobody in the audience noticed it, either. Just like they didn't see your mistake."

The older lady helped Kiki tuck in one of the ends of her head wrap, then they left the restroom.

Wow. They had messed up and nobody even knew it. How cool was that? Even their mistakes looked good.

Alonzo offered me and Daddy a ride home, so we didn't get to ride on the train. Alonzo was the driver, and I was expecting Tameka to sit up front with him. But Daddy said his legs were too long to sit in the back, so Tameka ended up beside me in the back seat. *Please don't try to start a conversation*, I thought.

"How's the Double Dutch coming?" asked Tameka.

"Okay."

"Have you had any tournaments?"

"No."

"When I used to jump, we had tournaments. In fact, we had the April First Double Dutch Jump-Off every year."

"April first is April Fool's Day. That sounds stupid."

"It was fantastic. They still do it every year, although not as many schools participate like they used to. I bet if your school did it, you'd have a decent chance at winning."

"I guess."

I didn't like talking to Tameka, but I did like the idea of a Double Dutch tournament. In fact, I would love to be in a Double Dutch tournament. I could see me winning a hundred prizes. I'd be like the African dancer girl, with everybody thinking I'm the best person in the whole place and everybody looking at me. I'd have that stage-presence thing down pat as soon as I learned how to get it.

When we got back home, we found Mom watching TV. Something about a husband and wife and a detective and a lot of arguing going on. It was a yawn of a show—to me, anyway. But Mom was deep into it.

"Mom?" I was waiting for the commercial, and as soon as it started, I said, "Mom, when are we going to jump rope again?"

"Didn't you tell me you joined a team at school?"

"Yes, but I mean *you*. When are *you* going to jump some more?"

"Girl, it's February, the coldest month on the calendar. It's entirely too frigid outside for me to go jumping Double Dutch in the middle of some parking lot."

"You could come to my school and jump," I said. "You'd be a better advisor than Ms. McMillan. She's in charge of our team, but she doesn't even know how to do Double Dutch. We have to come up with everything ourselves."

My mother had already tuned me out. Her show had come back on, and she was all into some lady who had killed her husband and it looked like she was going to get away with it. I waited for the next commercial to come on. It was for diarrhea medicine.

"Mom, what's worse: diarrhea or hypertension?"

"What are you talking about?"

"What's a worse sickness to have: diarrhea or hypertension?"

"You don't want either one of them. What's wrong? Are you sick?"

"No, I was just wondering if…" All of a sudden, I was scared to ask her about her condition. She was looking at me with a face I couldn't read.

"At Cousin Julia's, I heard you say you were going to start dieting. And exercising."

"Yeah…"

"Have you started yet?"

"Well…I've been thinking about it."

"But you haven't started doing it. Why don't you start doing Double Dutch with me? We could be in a tournament and everything!"

"Maybe I can visit your school one day to see you jump."

"You think you want to volunteer to be one of the adult helpers?"

"No, Jayla. You know I work every day! There's no way I can budget time to volunteer at your school. I'll just come and visit one time. Would you like that?"

I nodded yes, and I headed for the stairs. She called after me. "But if you need an adult to volunteer with the team on a regular basis, maybe you could ask Tameka to help out."

Tameka? No thanks. I'll stick to silly old Ms. McMillan.

CHAPTER 10

From then on, I carried my rope around with me everywhere just in case Mom changed her mind. But usually when we went anywhere, it was just the two of us—at the grocery store, the drugstore, the mall—and you need at least three people to play. Then one day after work, Mom picked up Cousin Julia, and we went to the Fitness Regimen Studio. It was a cold February evening, but I asked if I could ride with them just to get out of the house. Cousin Julia had convinced my mother that they needed to exercise and that maybe a gym membership would help. They were going to check it out.

"Welcome to Fitness Regimen Studio," said a very handsome man. He wasn't all that tall, but he stood straight like a telephone pole. His shirt was tight against his body almost like he had a second skin on top of his regular skin. It made you look at the muscles on his arms and in his chest. He spoke like a sergeant in charge of soldiers. "Fitness Regimen Studio—the facility to make your future fit." This same sentence was printed on a large silver sign with black lettering as you entered the lobby area. The machines were black and silver, the carpet was charcoal gray, and the walls were painted a cloudy white. Mom's red coat, Cousin Julia's tan coat and brown boots, and my navy parka were the most colorful things in the place.

"Good evening," my mother said. She paused as she looked around. So did I. There were lots of different kinds of equipment all around the place. Bicycles bolted to the floor with people pedaling in place. Long cords suspended from poles that people pulled back and forth while seated on padded benches. I saw a woman who moved like she was rowing a boat, but she was sitting on the floor. The only person not clamped onto a contraption was a man way on the other side of the gym who was jumping rope the way boxers do when they train. Nobody was talking and most people wore headphones. Everybody looked serious, maybe even in pain.

Nobody seemed to be having fun. In PE class at school, we got excited. "Pass me the ball!" "Yay, it's my turn!" "Nice shot." "Hooray, we won!" Even with something as plain and simple as when Maya and I would race each other to the end of the block or play a game on the Wii, we would compliment or congratulate each other. "Hey, you've gotten faster!" "You made the point. Good job." "Girl, you were flying down the street—even though I still beat you!" Wow, I missed Maya.

Despite all the shiny machines, this gym seemed dim and grim to me. No wonder grown-ups got fat when they grew up if this was what it meant to exercise.

"At Fitness Regimen, we believe that the formula for success is frame, form, and frequency." The man sounded like the kind of voice programmed into a virtual assistant. "Frame refers to the set of exercises and the necessary equipment to do the workout. Form is the proper way in which you execute the workout. And frequency is the number of times you work out."

"Can we take a look around?" Mom asked.

"Minors are not allowed on the gym floor," he said, staring down his nose in my direction. Somehow, he didn't look as handsome to me anymore. "She would have to stay here. And be supervised by an adult. So if one of you would like to come with me, and one stays behind, I can show you the studio."

This man had the opposite of stage presence. He had proper posture and proper speech but nothing drew you to him. He looked good, but it didn't feel good to be around him. He had the frame and the form, but he transmitted on a highly negative frequency.

My mom followed behind Mr. Android while Cousin Julia and I stayed back and waited on some bony black and silver seats. I got restless, so I took out my clothesline and doubled it so that I could jump solo.

Cousin Julia gave me a look and at first I thought she was going to tell me to stop. But instead she said, "I wish I could jump, too."

I stopped midjump. "Okay, go ahead and jump," I said and handed over the rope. Cousin Julia unzippered her boots, peeled off her knee socks. She took the rope and started jumping by herself in her bare feet.

"Sure does get the blood pumping," she gasped in between jumps, but she was grinning. After going for a good clip, she stopped and said, "But what I really want to do is Double Dutch."

That's what I really wanted to do, too. But I didn't say anything. I just handed her the ends, I took the other ends, and we started turning. Inside my head, I was praying Mom would come back and start jumping.

Instead, a man with a potbelly ran over. He was laughing as he ran up to us and jumped *at* the rope, not in it, clearly wanting to joke around and not really jump.

"Can I jump rope? Nope, nope, nope!" he quipped.

"Come on, we can get you jumping if you really want to," said Cousin Julia. "Just do like this." Cousin Julia demonstrated a bunny hop, had him do it a few times outside the rope, then positioned him in the middle of the rope. We starting turning and he started jumping. He did real good, too. He did a bunch of jumping jacks and was so happy and surprised that he was able to actually do it that he missed due to laughing so hard, not because he wasn't able.

"Let me try it." The man who jumped rope like a boxer had come over. He didn't want to stand in the middle of the rope and be coached how to jump. He wanted to jump in with the ropes in motion.

"When this rope goes up, you go in," Cousin Julia told him. "And aim for the center."

He watched the ropes with deep concentration, waiting for that space where the rope opened up. He took his time, and he timed it right, diving into the rope like an arrow aiming for its mark. He had such a rapid pace that Cousin Julia and I had to pick up our turning pace to keep up with him. He jumped for a long time. People started drifting over to watch. Several people pulled out their phones to film him.

"He's good!" "Wow, check that out!" "Look at that—I haven't seen Double Dutch in years." I heard people's admiring comments. Then out of the corner of my eye, I saw a red blur rush past me and leap into the rope. It was my mother. She jumped in with the Boxer Guy, matching his step.

"Stay where you are. Don't move," I heard her say to him in a loud whisper. Then she did the move I had seen on YouTube. She jumped around to the front of him and grabbed his hands so they were perfectly in sync. Then she said, "Follow my lead," and she led him in turning around together as they held hands. They almost made it completely around in a circle, but then they missed.

It didn't matter, though. The people who were watching—and everybody was watching, even the people who were still working out on the machines—broke out into applause.

The whole atmosphere in the studio switched. It changed from February to June, from a funeral service to a wedding celebration. Where it had at first felt cold, dead, and colorless, now the room had come to life. Mom said, "Keep turning," and she jumped back in. This time, after she established her rhythm, she turned to Julia and said, "Pick it up. I'm going to do my pop up."

Cousin Julia yelled, "*Turn*, Jayla!" so I turned faster and harder, and then Mom shot up high in the rope and came back down in rhythm. Next, she did a series of pop ups and probably would've done ten more if the Android Man hadn't run over yelling, "That is unauthorized! Double Dutch is not permitted." He glared hard at the customers who had gathered around us. I could tell by the look on their faces that they were disappointed; I knew some of them would've joined in if he'd let them. But they moved away and we stopped turning. He gave Cousin Julia a long stare starting with her bare feet. "Health regulations require shoes at all times," he said.

"I'm getting my socks and shoes and my hat and coat," she said as she hurriedly pulled herself together. "Let's go, Sherry, Jayla."

"I didn't like the place at first, but jumping Double Dutch made it fun!" I said as soon as we got out the door. The February air was so cold it was like a slap to the face, but after being in the closed-up, sweat-soaked air of the fitness facility, it was almost a relief.

"That was weird," my mother said. "I don't think I want to go there again. That man's attitude was so nasty."

"He must spray himself with people-repellent," I said and shivered, not quite sure if it was because of the temperature or the thought of that man.

Cousin Julia was busy rebuttoning her coat. She had been in such a hurry to leave she hadn't bundled up properly. A few flakes of snow were beginning to fall and the night was frigid. "You got that right, honey. If baloney were snow, he'd be a blizzard," she said. "But you know what the worst part was?"

"No, what?" I turned to face Cousin Julia before we got in the car. She sighed a heavy sigh.

"I didn't get a chance to jump Double Dutch."

CHAPTER 11

Tuesday was the first of March. As I walked to school, I wondered why they called this month March. It's still too cold to be outdoors marching anywhere. June would be a better month for marching outdoors. Or even September or October, when marching bands are playing music and displaying their school colors. Spring starts in March, but the weather doesn't match up with spring on most days. It's all wishy-washy, bouncing between winter and semi-spring, until the very, very end of the month when you get a day or two of warm weather.

Today was a Marchy day. It was chilly and a bit foggy, but I didn't mind because it was Tuesday and that meant Double Dutch practice. But first, I had to get through the school day. Usually on Tuesdays, I couldn't wait till class let out and I could go jump rope. But today, Mr. Kurata taught something pretty interesting.

We were studying the human skeleton. The picture of the skeleton in the book creeped me out a little. It reminded me of scary movies and crawly creatures and death and dying. But once we started talking about it, my feelings shifted. I could see how amazing all the bones and muscles in our bodies are.

I learned a new term: synovial joint. Your knees, elbows, and shoulders are all synovial joints. That means they're movable joints coated with a slippery liquid called *synovial fluid*. I liked the word *synovial* because it rhymed with *jovial*. And jovial is how I felt when I used my synovial joints to jump.

Mr. Kurata's PowerPoint presentation showed an X-ray of the foot and the caption read "A human foot has 100 muscles, ligaments, and tendons."

I wiggled my toes inside my shoes. There were 100 different things inside of there? The next slide had a cartoon picture of ten toes and it read: "Your big toe has two bones. The other toes have three bones each."

"What do you call a ghost with a broken foot? A hobbling goblin!" Jade called out. A bunch of people laughed and even more groaned. The next slide said, "The average person will take about 200 million steps in their lifetime."

Two hundred million! A Double Dutch kid probably does at least one million steps at practice. That made me ask a question. "Mr. Kurata, I jump Double Dutch. Do you think that changes how my bones work?"

"Jumping rope probably makes your bones stronger," said Mr. Kurata. "Exercise is a good prescription for almost any condition." He had Jade google facts about exercising and read them out loud.

"The following are benefits of exercise for youth," Jade read. "Children who exercise have leaner, slimmer bodies."

I saw Kierra look up and take note. She wanted to be a model when she grew up.

"And have stronger muscles and bones," Jade continued, and I saw Davon do a bicep curl. "Better academics." Mr. Kurata cleared his throat meaningfully and gave each of us a significant look. "Lower blood pressure." I needed to tell Mom that one. "And increased opportunity for socializing." Huh. Maybe I'd make a whole lot of friends and wouldn't need my crazy family if I kept up Double Dutch.

After class, I asked Jade and Kierra if they wanted to check it out. They told me they were going to the coloring club after school. I asked a couple of other classmates, and they said no, too. But I didn't let that discourage me. *I* was going to Double Dutch, and for now, that was good enough for me.

I was feeling pretty good—pretty jovial—because I wanted to tell Ms. McMillan and the other kids about the Double Dutch contest. I had googled "April First Double Dutch Jump-Off." It was for kids all over the metro DC area. Maybe Ms. McMillan would let us compete. It might even get some of the kids who dropped out to come back to practice.

Actually, I think Ms. McMillan might have been the reason some of the kids had dropped out. I think kids were allergic to her. The first person she affected was a girl named Taylor. She said Ms. McMillan made Double Dutch too boring. Next to go was a boy named Kim. I asked him why he didn't come back, and he said he liked basketball better. But I think it was all over for him the day he was offering a suggestion he got from the basketball coach that he thought we could try, but he caught Ms. McMillan looking off in the distance like she wasn't paying attention. "Are you listening to me?" he'd asked. And Ms. McMillan said, "Just one minute, let me take care of this first." Then she rummaged through her purse looking for something. Next, she wandered over to the volleyball coach to ask a question. After that, she walked out of the gymnasium completely, leaving Kim hanging like a button on a thrift store shirt.

Next, it was Terrie who left—and she was such a good jumper! Ms. McMillan had a book with names of all the students enrolled in the after-school activities. One day, Terrie saw the book had been left open. There were two Terries at our school, and to tell them apart, Ms. McMillan had made a note beside the name of one of them. In parentheses was the word *homely*. Terrie wasn't sure which Terrie Ms. McMillan meant, but once she saw that she was through.

So we were down to me, Davon, and Nia. I was good, Davon was strong, but Nia turned rope like she had wet noodles for arms and she jumped rope like she was scared to put her feet on the floor. She still moved like a beginner even though it had been nearly three months. Yet Ms. McMillan always told Nia she was "Doing fine, doing fine, yes. You're doing beautifully."

Ms. McMillan was always saying the wrong nice thing to the right person and saying the right mean thing to the wrong nice person. Because of her, my Double Dutch team was just three measly people. We didn't even have a name. So I decided that at Tuesday's practice, we'd pick out a name for our team.

"Ms. McMillan, can we enter a contest?"

"Contest? For what?"

"A Double Dutch contest. Kids from all over the city will be in it."

"When is it? And where?"

I showed her the colorful flyer I had printed out on my

computer at home. It had drained all my ink but I figured it was worth it. If we won, maybe more kids would join and kids would come back. Maybe someone would take our pictures and stream us live on YouTube. Everybody would see me on the Internet. I'd end up being watched by kids all over the country just like I had watched those Double Dutch girls online at Thanksgiving. I'd be famous!

"So can we enter?"

"Let me see, let me see," Ms. McMillan said, reaching for her tablet. She stared at the blank screen for a long time.

"Aren't you going to turn it on?"

"I can't remember my password. It was something simple. I made it easy so I could remember it, and now I forgot."

For weeks, she'd forgotten to bring her tablet and now that she had remembered, she'd forgotten the password.

"I bet I could log you on, Ms. McMillan," I offered. "What's your birth date?"

"April 1," she said. *No wonder*, I thought.

I punched in 0401 and her tablet opened right up. I showed her the tournament website.

"Yes, yes, I see there are four requirements." Ms. McMillan began reciting the rules out loud. "Each team has to be composed of at least four people, all students from the same—oh, I can read this later."

"What else does it say?" I wanted to know what I had to do.

114

"Let's see, let me see—lost my place. Here it is. Have a team name and a team captain. Teams are judged in three categories: freestyle, compulsories—whatever that is—"

"It's the jump rope basics," I told her.

"Yes, yes—and stage presence."

There was that *stage presence* thing again. Yeah, I needed to nail that down. That was the right stuff.

I peered over Ms. McMillan's shoulder. The prizes were a trophy, a T-shirt, and a video of your team's routine.

I'd rather have a big, fat gold trophy over an itty-bitty gold ring. If we won a trophy, we'd be TTC—too totally cool. Mr. Washington would announce our names over the PA, our team trophy would be displayed in the big glass case at the front of the school, and our pictures would be all over social media. I'd send links of it to everybody I knew—or at least I would if I had my own phone. I could probably get Shontessa to send stuff for me.

Meanwhile, Ms. McMillan was looking over the tournament website.

"Ms. McMillan, can we compete in this?"

"Yes, yes. At least I think so—probably yes. When is the April First Double Dutch Jump-Off?"

"It's April first." I wanted to say more but I kept my mouth shut.

"Oh, yes, yes, that's right. That's my birthday." Ms.

McMillan looked around the room at the three of us. "We need to get some of the old kids who started with us to come back."

"And we need to come up with a team name," I said.

"Yes, yes, let's think up a name," Ms. McMillan said, agreeing.

"Name the team after me!" Davon said. "Davon and the Double Dutch Backup Girls."

"I like that name," said Nia, grinning big at Davon.

"No way!" I shouted. Davon was jumping up and down and throwing his fists like he was a boxer on a pogo stick. I turned to him. "Davon, I know you want to compete, but the team isn't all about you."

"I can outjump anybody—boy or girl. Even you, Jayla," he bragged.

"You can't do better than me."

"Sure I can. You don't even have a stunt. I can jump fast, spin around, and do pop ups. My Running Man is the joint!"

"I know how to turn around in the rope," I protested. I could do a pop up, too, although I wasn't able to jump as high as he could.

Davon laughed and said, "Anybody can turn around. Even Nia can do that."

At least Nia kept coming back every Tuesday for practice. But Davon was right. I needed a show-stopping move.

"Let's just jump," I said. April was exactly thirty days away. I had a feeling that the other teams had been practicing all school year long.

Nia went first. Ms. McMillan and Davon did the turning. She started off slow. I started a chant to help her get her rhythm up.

"I like coffee. I like tea. I like the boys and the boys like me. A. B. C. D."

She missed on the letter D. "So who is your true love, Nia?" I teased her. But she acted like she didn't hear me. She was staring at Davon. Maybe that's why she missed so easily—she was too busy crushing on Davon. She never paid attention. She was probably going to grow up to be another Ms. McMillan.

"Davon, it's your turn," Nia said softly. Ms. McMillan and I were turning for him. I knew my arms were going to get a real workout because Davon had endless energy. He didn't need us to chant to get him going; we just counted his steps while he jumped and prayed our arms didn't fall off before he missed. It made me mad that Nia was just standing there watching while I was doing all the work. She hadn't turned yet. I dropped the rope.

"Nia, you can turn for a while."

She stared at me blankly for a second, then went over to pick up the rope. Davon gave me a look, too, as if to say,

Why'd you quit on me? But he didn't say anything and got back into his groove once she started turning. It wasn't long before he messed up because Nia couldn't turn worth a dime.

"Children, children, it looks like you've gotten tired. Let's call it a day. We'll practice next Tuesday."

"We're not finished!" I protested. "And we haven't come up with a name." But Ms. McMillan was rolling up the rope and Nia was following Davon out of the gym.

This practice was a dud. Our dinky little team was in no way ready for a Double Dutch competition with contestants from all over the city. Life was so unfair. Even though I hadn't done anything to mess things up, things that were not my fault were messing me up: the fact that Nia couldn't jump and, oh yeah, that we still needed one more person to be on the team.

I wanted to do the tournament. I wanted to show people I had stage presence. I wanted to be a star on the Internet. I'd even put up with someone I didn't like if they could help me do that. Who could I get who could jump well, who could show off in the rope, and who could help me get seen on the Internet?

Shontessa.

CHAPTER 12

I love to run. Maya and I used to race each other to the corner all the time. Even now, sometimes when I was going from a store to the car or crossing a parking lot or walking from the house to the curb, I'd have an urge to say, "Race ya!"

The words in my head must've jumped out of my mouth 'cause next thing I know, Mom sprinted off. She had just parked the car and we'd both gotten out. She had surprised me by picking me up after the Tuesday practice—she'd left work early for a doctor's appointment. The weather was a bit chilly but not too bad, so Ms. McMillan had held Double Dutch practice outdoors. Mom had watched us for a few minutes.

"You really are good!" she had said, and it made me feel happy down to the tips of my toes to hear. Actually, I

thought I was pretty good, but it meant a lot to have someone who really knew all about Double Dutch to say so. "If
you keep it up, I bet you could compete—and win!" she said
as she walked me from the playground to our Honda. A stiff
wind blew and pushed us down the sidewalk. "Oh, I miss
my days of Double Dutch," she said, jingling the car keys.
"Not only did we jump in the gym at school, we jumped
on the playground at the rec center and on the sidewalk
at home."

"So why'd you stop?"

"Oh, I don't know. I guess when you become an adult
you figure you're not supposed to play anymore." The wind
picked up again and made a sound like a gasp. Or maybe the
gasp was from Mom.

"Not supposed to play? You mean once you get grown
you're not allowed to have fun?"

She turned on the ignition, and the engine strained for
a minute before it finally turned over. "Now that certainly
doesn't sound right," she said. I wasn't sure if she meant the
car or my comment. She didn't say anything more until we
pulled up in front of the house. And that's when I must've
accidentally said the words "Race ya!" and Mom took off—
and beat me. We both laughed as she unlocked the door and
we tumbled into the house, breathing hard and spilling over
each other.

She was beaming. Her face had a warm glow about it. I bet that short run had her synovial joints, her feet, maybe even her mind feeling jovial. Maybe that good feeling would work in my favor.

"Will you come back to school and jump with me next week?"

"No, Jayla. I can't budget time into my schedule to go to your school every Tuesday."

"What about jumping rope at home?"

She dropped her keys in the dish at the door, then thought for a moment. "Hmmm...I could certainly jump solo." I could see the idea move across her face as it worked itself through her brain.

"Maybe if we tied the rope to the fence, you and I could do Double Dutch in the backyard," she said.

I wanted to shout "Yes!" but decided to keep quiet as she made her way to yes by herself.

"And maybe Shontessa could come by sometimes after school or on the weekends to jump with us." She stared off as if she was picturing the Double Dutch session. "I could show you girls some stunts," she added.

I was thrilled to hear that. Even the part about adding Shontessa to the mix sounded good, since I wanted her to be in the upcoming tournament.

I thought about asking Mom about her doctor's

appointment. Was her high blood pressure getting better? Or had nothing changed? I wanted to ask but was a little afraid to find out the answer. I thought about a text conversation I had seen Mom having with Big Lucy. Last night just before we had started dinner, Mom had left her phone out and I had picked it up. I saw what she had been texting.

Lucy
Hey, Sherry. Give me a ride 2morrow @noon?

Sherry
No. Follow-up Doc appt to check high blood pressure. Last time my pressure was 150/90.

Lucy
That's high! My doc said I have to bring my #s down, too.

Sherry
Doc keeps saying exercise. But gym membership - no can do.

Lucy
We need to do something.

Sherry
Maybe I'll just have to take more pills.

Lucy
My ride is here. CU L8R.

Why was it so hard for Mom and Big Lucy to exercise? At school they made us do PE once a week and we had recreational activities after school every day. Couldn't she do the same thing at work?

And if her doctor was bugging her to exercise and she didn't do it, then what would happen? Would she get sicker?

In third grade, Hermie the hamster looked fine and normal on a Tuesday. Then on Wednesday, our teacher, Mrs. Hamilton, announced he was dead. I was so shocked. The day before I had played with Hermie and he was running around like nothing was wrong. Then, *boom*. There he was, stiff and dead in his hamster cage. Were humans and hamsters alike, appearing healthy one minute but sick to death the next?

I had thought I might bring up the subject tonight after dinner, but Mom left to go to a community meeting. It was me and Daddy washing dishes.

"Do you think Mom's high blood pressure is real bad?" I asked Daddy while his back was turned to me. He was loading the dishwasher. I was rinsing the plates.

"No, not if she does what the doctor tells her to do."

"What's that?" I turned off the faucet so I could hear his answer.

"The same thing it is for most health problems—eat right and exercise."

"That doesn't sound so hard."

"It's simple. But not necessarily easy." I passed a pan to Daddy, but he handed it back. "You need to rinse this one again."

"What's so hard about it?"

"Well, it's easier to chill out than to work out."

"It's not that hard. And why call it 'working out'? Working out makes it sound like, well, *work*. When it's something that's good, it should be called play."

"You need to rinse this one again," he repeated. He pointed to the nasty, crusty stuff still stuck on the frying pan.

"It's too hard to get off. Why can't the dishwasher do it?"

"Are you saying it's too much work?" Daddy asked with his eyebrow raised.

"This *is* work. Scrubbing crud off pots and pans isn't fun."

"If I called it the Dishwashing Game, would that make it fun?"

Calling a workout play was one thing because exercising was definitely fun. Calling dishwashing a game did not make scrubbing cruddy pots and pans anything other than disgusting. I filled the pan with soapy water to let it soak and decided to change the subject.

"Daddy, will Alonzo still do Niece Night after he gets married?"

"Maybe not as often at first, but you'll still be special to him. Just because he loves Tameka doesn't mean he doesn't still love you."

"But when Maya left, we kept in touch for a little while, and now we don't talk at all." All of a sudden, it felt like a glob was sitting in the middle of my throat. I swallowed a few times, then said in a small voice, "I'm afraid the same thing's going to happen with Cousin Alonzo."

"Sometimes life is like that. That's why it's important to keep up with the people in your circle."

"Did you stop hanging with Alonzo when you and Mom got married?"

"At first, I was spending a lot time with Sherry, but eventually me and Alonzo picked it up where we left off."

"Was Alonzo mad at you for being with Mom?"

"No, he understood. He knows we're always gonna be family. Sherry was just someone extra added to the circle. More folks to love makes our family bigger and better and more interesting."

"More folks makes things more complicated."

"Complicated in a good way. Look, you love Niece Night, right? Uncle Javon invented Nephew Night. Aunt Stacie inspired Niece Night, and Alonzo took it to a new level. By the time he and Tameka have kids, you'll probably have a new twist to the family traditions."

"Yeah, I'm going to invent Double Dutch Day."

"DDD—I think it should stand for Daughter, Do the Dishes." And he handed me another crusty pot to clean.

———

Double Dutch felt more like flying than flying in an airplane.

When I think of flying, I think *whoosh, zoom, zip*. I'd only ridden on an airplane once when I was little. I had been excited about the trip, but it had turned out not so exciting. We had a real early flight, so I was barely awake going to the airport. As soon as we got seated, I fell asleep and missed takeoff. Once we were in the sky, I woke up toward the end of the flight and looked out the window. I saw clouds floating beneath us, and that was pretty cool, but it didn't feel like we were moving much. I fell back asleep and when I woke up again we were back on the ground.

But Double Dutch—now *that* was flying. Especially once Mom taught me how to jump in the rope. You stand on the side at "the door" waiting for that right moment to go. Mom explained that when the rope nearest me is at its highest point, that's the time I jump in. But that moment wasn't just a time and space calculation for when to jump in, she said. You had to feel it.

And that's how I knew when to go for it. It felt like a wind grabbed me and carried me into the rope when the time was right. It was like riding a wave, but instead of plunging into a pool, I was launching into the air. Propelling myself up and down felt like an explosion of glitter. My body was so happy I couldn't contain myself. It made me understand the term *jumping for joy* or how some people in church *get happy* and start dancing in the aisles.

Of course, some of what Mom taught me was just plain and ordinary stuff, like learning how to count your steps or do compulsories or how not to be double-handed. Nothing was worse than being double-handed. That was when you turned the rope lopsided. But I still thought all of that plain and ordinary stuff was awesome.

Mom and I were doing jump rope one Saturday afternoon. The March sun played hide-and-seek with the clouds. Sometimes we were bathing in sunshine while we jumped; the next minute we were shivering in the shade. The back-and-forth weather fit my state of mind.

"Do I have to?"

"Yes, Jayla."

"Why can't you do it, Mom?"

"You're the one who wants it."

Shontessa was on her way over to join us. I had yet to ask her to be on the Taylor School Double Dutch team. She was a better all-around jumper than Nia or even Davon. Even better than me if I told the truth. She showed up in the backyard wearing skinny jeans, a short jacket with a thousand zippers on it, and high-top tennis shoes. Everything was in shades of turquoise and teal with flashes of red. Her earrings were the shape of lightning bolts—long, red, and dangly. She looked like a rapper about to rock the mic.

"Shontessa, you wanna jump rope?"

"That's why we're here."

"No, I mean for my school. There's a Double Dutch tournament next month. We want you on the team."

"How much am I going to be paid?"

"Nobody's getting paid, Shontessa." This girl was so impossible.

"Am I going to be on Instagram or YouTube? And what about that new one—*yo!*photo?"

"Yes, there's going to be social media. And if we win, they give us a trophy."

"Do I get my very own trophy? You know my moves are vicious. After all, I'm the one that will get you to first place."

"Nobody gets the trophy. It goes in the school's display case."

"That sucks. Will you have somebody to do my hair and makeup? And what are we wearing? Do I get a Double Dutch outfit?"

"Shontessa, I don't know the answers to all these crazy questions! Will you do it or not?" I put both hands on my hips and gave her a look.

She flipped her fake hair off the side of her face and swung it over her shoulder as she thought about her response.

"I guess." Shontessa said that like she was doing me such a big favor. And she was. But still.

"I'll play on your team. I want to be the lead dancer."

Mom unrolled the rope and handed an end to Shontessa.

"Shontessa, there is no lead dancer, no star, nothing like that," Mom told her. "It's just jump rope. And yes, you're good, but don't let it go to your head."

"Hmmph. You know you like my stuff."

"I like you better the less I see you," I said.

"You know I rock the rope. I could teach you a few things. In fact, I should be the team coach." She was working her neck like her head was on a trampoline. "I wonder if that's a thang—a rock coach."

"Cockroach is more like it."

"Girls! Enough of that." Mom handed the other end of the rope to me. "Are we going to fight, or are we going to jump?"

That ended the arguing. For the moment. Mom jumped first, then Shontessa took a turn in her blingin' outfit and with her dope dance moves. I hated to give her props but she really was off-the-hook in the rope.

So Shontessa would be a part of the team. That made me feel better. And worse.

CHAPTER 13

It took a whole year. *No, I think it took five years. No, it was* a ten-year wait from the beginning of March to the beginning of April. At least that's how I felt waiting for April 1 and the April First Double Dutch Jump-Off.

That morning, as I was getting ready for school, I told my mom how nervous I was. "Suppose I mess up? Suppose I forget what to do?"

"You've been practicing a lot, both at school and at home," Mom said. "I can't believe you actually got me to jump outside in this chilly March weather with you."

It was true. We rehearsed nearly every other day after she came home from work. The agreement was that if she jumped rope with me, then I'd help her get dinner ready. Thanks to Alonzo, I knew a little bit about cooking, but she usually just had me make a salad. We used to only eat salads now and then. Now we had salad almost every night. At least every Double Dutch night.

"If your brain temporarily spaces out, your body will remember," Mom said. "That's called 'muscle memory.' Now finish your breakfast."

Who could eat scrambled eggs when your brain was scrambled eggs? But I went ahead and ate them anyway. Mom was having oatmeal with some walnuts and dates chopped up in it. She had stopped eating bacon and eggs for breakfast most days. She said not eating the bacon helped her think more clearly. I liked eggs, so I didn't mind not having the bacon that often anymore, but I missed the way it smelled as it sizzled in the skillet. The aroma of bacon in the morning almost makes it worth getting out of a warm bed.

"I think if I remember everything I'm supposed to do and Davon does his pop ups and Nia just doesn't mess up and Shontessa does her stunt—I think, I really think, we could win a prize."

"Don't concentrate on the prize. Concentrate on having a good time. Relax. It's your first competition," she told me. But how could I have a good time? How could I relax? After all, it was my very first competition!

Daddy had told me pretty much the same thing last night, but he was gone before I got up this morning. He was going to a conference in Baltimore and had to leave early to make the long drive. But he'd left me a note: "Jayla, jump to it! Remember to enjoy yourself and you'll be fine. Daddy."

As soon as I got to school, I looked for Davon. He was on the playground hanging around a group of boys. As usual, he was wearing his black high-top tennis shoes. Those were his favorites. Because he looked good—and jumped good—in his black sneakers and because we didn't have uniforms, we had decided to wear all black. I brought a pair of black shorts and a black T-shirt that I would change into after school. Wearing all black made me feel like a Double Dutch ninja.

"You ready for the tournament, Davon?" I said.

"I'm ready like Freddy, steady like Eddie, but not sweaty like Betty," rapped Davon. All his little friends laughed. I smirked at him and kept on going. Walking the hallway toward my classroom, I looked around for Nia. She was at her locker and she was wearing her lucky earrings. They were a bright bubblegum pink and really stood out against the black top and black pants she wore.

I was glad I wouldn't see Ms. McMillan until after school. Her scatterbrain-headedness would only make me more nervous.

At lunchtime, I got Nia to text Shontessa. Nia had a phone; I still didn't. Shontessa responded and let us know she would meet us at the front of our school building and Ms. McMillan would drive all of us to the April First Double Dutch Jump-Off. Mom was going to meet us at the tournament site. I was excited for her to see me do all the things we had practiced at home—and in front of a big crowd! I thought she would be proud of me. All afternoon I felt like I was hanging on to the monkey bars with greasy fingers. It seemed like I was going to fall off the edge at any moment. I wished the afternoon would hurry and go by and I was scared that it would get here too soon.

Finally, class was over. I ran to the gym to meet up with Nia and Davon. Davon had a short single rope and was jumping like a prizefighter getting ready for a bout. Nia was sitting on a stool—the one Ms. McMillan usually used—and spinning herself around and around. But Ms. McMillan wasn't there.

"Where's Ms. McMillan?"

"I haven't seen her," Nia said, and she gave herself another spin on the stool.

Maybe she was in the principal's office. I went down the hall to Mr. Washington's office. I had to wait awhile because he had somebody's parents in his office. Glad it wasn't me who was in trouble. I asked the secretary if I could wait. She waved her hand at me in a gesture I figured meant yes while she continued her conversation on the phone.

While I was waiting, Shontessa arrived. *Good.* She'd remembered to wear all black, I was glad to see. She had on a black T-shirt with a short black skirt, but her tennis shoes had neon green laces and she wore hair ribbons and earrings and about ten bracelets in the same eye-shocking shade.

"I came inside 'cause I got tired of waiting for you all outdoors. You ready?" Shontessa said.

"I'm a little nervous," I admitted. "This is my first time ever being in a competition. What about you?"

"I look good so I'll probably do good." Shontessa. Always bragging. "What's wrong with you that you're so scared?"

"Why do I bother to ask you anything? Maybe Ms. McMillan will have something nice to say to me."

"Ms. McMillan isn't here today," the secretary said, hanging up the phone and butting into our conversation.

"What? She's supposed to be taking us to the April First Double Dutch Jump-Off!" I felt like my heart had stopped.

"Well, she isn't here and won't be here all day." The secretary was tapping on her keyboard, looking all unconcerned like this news was no big deal. "She called out because today is her birthday."

"There's got to be some mistake!" How could she forget that today was an important day? "She's supposed to be our ride!"

"She isn't coming in. I took the call myself," the secretary said. "She said she was taking off to celebrate her birthday.

In fact, she said she was going out to lunch *and* to dinner." She looked up from her computer at my shocked face. "You want to call your mother for a ride?" The secretary pointed to the fat, square office phone squatting on the desk beside her. I lunged at it like it was the last Oreo in the cookie jar.

"Oh no. Oh no. Oh no," I kept moaning while I waited for Mom to pick up the phone. My first chance to be a star and because of Ms. Amnesia McMillan I was going to lose it. Out to lunch—she was literally out to lunch *and* dinner. Ms. McMillan was too ditzy to be believed. She was ruining my whole life!

"Mom! Mom!" I wailed. I couldn't get any other words out.

"What's wrong with her?" asked the secretary, looking at Shontessa.

"Jayla, are you all right?" I could hear the concern in Mom's voice, but I couldn't get anything else out. Every time I thought about how Ms McMillan had betrayed me, I got mad and sad and tongue-tied.

"Jayla, calm down," said Shontessa. She walked over and took the phone from me.

I couldn't help myself. For the last three months, I had tried so hard to get a team going and now it was all going bust because silly Ms. McMillan had blown us off to celebrate her ridiculous birthday.

"Hi, Aunt Sherry," I heard Shontessa saying into the

phone. "The teacher in charge called out, so we don't have a ride to the Double Dutch tournament. Jayla's kirking out about it."

Shontessa was silent for a long minute, then said, "OK," and hung up.

"Why'd you hang up?" I screamed at Shontessa. "I wanted to speak to her. What did she say?"

"Young lady, lower your voice!" said the secretary in a voice just as loud as mine.

"What did she say?" I insisted as I pulled on Shontessa's arm to lead her out of the office. Her fifty million neon bracelets were rattling way louder than my voice.

"Your mother's going to give us a ride," said Shontessa, like she wasn't at all worried about it. "Where are the other kids? You need to find them and get them all together."

I ran back to the gym to grab Nia and Davon. They were sitting on the bleachers watching some guys practicing free throws.

"Where's Ms. McMillan?" Nia asked when she saw me rush in.

"She's not here! She didn't come to school today. Can you believe she did that to us?" I spluttered.

"So we're not doing the tournament?" Nia asked.

"Yes, we're still doing it! My mother's coming to get us and drive us there."

"She got a big car?" Davon asked. And that thought stopped me the way a computer virus crashes a hard drive. Our Honda Civic was fine for me, Mom, and Daddy, but could Mom, me, Davon, Nia, and Shontessa all fit? Well, we *had* to fit; we just absolutely *had* to. What else could we do?

I started walking up and down the side of the basketball court. We couldn't *not* show up. How could Ms. McMillan forget all about us like this?

"Wanna jump while we're waiting?" Davon asked.

I felt too jumpy to jump, but then I thought maybe jumping would calm me down until our ride showed up. We had just unraveled the rope when Shontessa sauntered in.

"Oh good!" she said. "I want to go."

And just like that, she jumped in before anybody else had a chance to even say anything. That girl made me so mad. But I didn't bother fussing at her because at least she was going to be on our team and she would help us win. Shontessa had great moves. She jumped using a lot of hip-hop dance moves, a few Beyoncé booty shakes and body rolls, then she'd close out with some leg shoots that were so fast and furious they made you think of flashing lights. A few times when she did that move, the guys on the court stopped playing ball and yell, "Shoop, shoop, shoop!" in sync with her movements. It was exciting to watch her.

After Shontessa's go, Nia jumped and surprisingly did

pretty well. I guess all that consistent practice finally paid off. Then Davon took a turn and lasted in the rope a long time. Finally it was my turn when the PA system announced, "Will Jayla from the Double Dutch team report to the office?"

I ran and left Nia, Shontessa, and Davon behind as I headed for the school office. The secretary held out the phone for me. It was Mom.

"My car is acting up. I called your father, but he won't be back from Baltimore till around seven tonight. What I'm going to do is catch Metro—"

"No, not Metro! It'll take forever and we'll get there too late!"

"You're right. I'll get an Uber to your school, round all of you up, and then catch another Uber to the tournament."

"Does Uber come in extra large?"

"What do you mean?"

"There's four of us, plus you. It needs to be a car with enough room."

"You're right." Mom was silent for a moment. "I guess I may have to book two cars." I could hear her adding up the cost in her head. "This wasn't in the budget..."

How were we going to get to the tournament? I couldn't believe this.

And that's when I remembered Tameka. And her huge SUV.

"Could you call Tameka?" I asked Mom meekly. "I bet she'd come get us."

Fifteen minutes later, a blue SUV pulled up in front of the building. I didn't say much on the ride. I was feeling some kind of way for quite a few reasons: Seeing Tameka. Not seeing Mom because of something having to do with getting the car towed. I was glad that Tameka showed up for us. But a little bit bothered because it *was* Tameka. I guess this is what had to happen in order to make things happen.

At least we were going.

CHAPTER 14

When we got to the April First Double Dutch Jump-Off (finally), it was in the largest gymnasium I had ever seen. It was at a huge senior high school and the gym was filled with kids from schools all over. It looked like there were a zillion teams competing. And they all had much cooler uniforms than what we were wearing. They had on actual outfits that matched and they were in team colors with the team name written on the back of them. Our plain black clothes made us look like we were orphans at a funeral.

"Why are you looking so sad? We're going to have some fun!" Tameka said.

"Look at their uniforms!" I protested. "They're stylin' so much better than us. We look like losers compared to them!"

Tameka gave me a pitying look and said, "You don't win based on how you dress. You win based on how you jump."

Shontessa and I both looked at each other when Tameka said that. We both knew that winners always look good. I know Tameka thought she knew what she was talking about, but I wasn't so sure.

"I like wearing all black. Plus, I know I've got the flyest moves!" Davon stated, strutting up to the registration table.

"Who's the adult sponsor?" asked the lady at the registration desk, looking past Davon at Tameka. When Tameka came forward, she handed her a form to fill out.

"Jayla, what's the name of your team?"

OMG! We had never decided on a team name. Now what were we going to do? We were disqualified before we even got in the door!

"Tameka, I don't know! We never came up with anything good. Are they going to put us out? Oh my God! I can't believe this is happen—"

"Calm down, Jayla. We'll just decide on a title for the team right now. Davon, Nia, any suggestions?" Tameka said, looking at the others.

Oh God, please don't let Davon name us. He'll name the team after himself. But it was Shontessa who spoke up first.

"Black *is* a fashion color. And we *are* hot. I know I am," she said. "So put the two together, and you've got Black Blaze."

And that's what Tameka wrote down. "I know the three of you go to Taylor Elementary. Shontessa, what's the name of your school?"

"Jefferson Middle School." And Tameka wrote that down along with our names and ages and some other information and handed the paper back to the registration lady.

"Black Blaze will be number thirteen in the lineup," she said. "Sit over there until it's your turn. You're the last team to perform."

The last team? I didn't know if I could sit still that long, waiting for twelve other teams to jump before we got a chance. And we were number thirteen? How unlucky could we get! I wanted it to hurry up and be over with. Watching everybody else would make me even more antsy than I already was.

Somebody blew a loud horn, then a voice came booming over the microphone telling everybody to be quiet. The person in charge said boring things about the history of the tournament and introduced some grown-ups who had something to do with something. Then the competition finally started.

The first four groups weren't *all that*. They did decent, but they didn't shine, and it gave me hope that maybe our team stood a chance. But then a team called the Bling Ring stepped up. They wore metallic gold capri pants and white shirts with gold trim around the collars. Plus, they had white baseball caps with each girl's name embroidered in gold on it. They wore the same gold earrings and they each had exactly two bracelets—one gold, one white—around their wrists. They even had the same hairdo: a ponytail that hung from the hole in the back of their caps. They looked so together, so perfectly matched up, I just knew they were going to be terrific.

My mouth really hung open once I saw them jump. They began with the compulsory moves that each team had to do. The tallest girl stumbled as she jumped into the rope and got her hand tangled and had to do it again. I know that cost them a lot of points. Another girl was a skillful speed jumper, but the rope skimmed her head and knocked her hat off and she missed while trying to fit the hat back on her head. Then when it was time for them to do some tricks, they didn't know any! They just jumped up and down for what seemed like a really long time. Nobody smiled. Watching them was like watching a hot pot of water cool off. Not much to see here. Yes, they were color coordinated, but they had no talent and no stage presence at all.

Tameka caught my eye. I think she knew what I was thinking. "All that glitters isn't gold," she said.

It gave me hope that Black Blaze wouldn't look like ashes when our turn finally came. As time went on, though, the teams got better and better. I was impressed by a group simply calling themselves the Grant School Double Dutch Team. They had uniforms, but they weren't new or fancy, just blue shorts and blue shirts that looked like they might have been their regular school gym uniform.

But boy, could they go!

"Did you see her?" Davon yelled, pointing to the team captain who had done a somersault into the rope. Everyone on the team did pop ups and everyone could skin the rope with ease. The stunt they did that I liked the best was when one girl and boy synchronized their steps, not just jumping up and down together, but doing a flip at exactly the same time and never missing a beat.

There was a team called Jump Fuzion who wore tie-dyed tops. They did a Running Man dance move that was cooler than anything I've ever seen on a music video. Then they got down low, like they were doing lunges, and jumped close to the ground.

"Look at that!" Davon yelled out again. Doing the Running Man was one of Davon's steps. I could see he was taking notes. I thought I could do that move myself. I thought maybe I could do both of those moves. They looked like a lot of fun.

After the seventh team competed, they called a halftime break. Tameka took me, Nia, Davon, and Shontessa into the hallway for a pep talk.

"You're going to go out there and do your best, guys!"

"Did you see that flip!" Davon said. "That was smokin'. I think I could do a flip like that."

"I can do a lunge *and* a flip," said Shontessa.

"Really?" I challenged her. "I've never seen you do it."

"I never did it before, but I think if I decided to, I could do one."

"I *know* I could do one," Davon repeated.

"Let's talk about what you already know how to do," Tameka said. "What's the plan?"

The plan was that Nia and Davon would start off doing the compulsory steps. Then, I'd get in the rope and do a few jumping jacks, turn around a few times, and do the C jump Mom had taught me in our backyard sessions. Then Shontessa and Davon would come back and do a stunt where they'd jump side by side, then weave from front-to-back and back-to-front around each other. Next, Shontessa would jump out and Davon would stay in the rope by himself and do his pop ups and his Running Man dance. Then he'd jump out and Shontessa would do her dance thing to top off our show. As much as I couldn't stand her, Shontessa was definitely the one we wanted closing out our routine.

A horn blared to signal that the competition was starting again, so we went back to the bleachers to watch the next five acts. Then it was our turn. My heart was thumping like a thunderbolt was trapped in my rib cage. I was afraid I wouldn't be able to move when the time came. The announcer shouted out, "From Taylor Elementary School, we have Black Blaze!"

And without me even thinking about what I was doing, I ran into position, taking up the ropes, and me and Shontessa were turning for Nia and Davon. I put all my attention on turning as good as I could. Most people don't know this, but the turner is as important as the jumper in making sure everything goes well. A good turner has to watch how the jumper moves and adjust her technique and tempo to the jumper's body.

Nia and Davon's compulsories seemed to go by in a flash, and next thing I knew, it was my turn to jump. I jumped in and did my jumping jacks, and Shontessa and Davon were turning with such a good rhythm that something took over my body. It felt like my body made the decision, not my mind. I did my C jump, and it flowed so easily I figured I'd do a second one, since I was feeling strong. On my second jump, it started off good, but when I came down, I didn't land on my foot the right way. I felt myself going down, so I just went with it and ended up jumping down low, bouncing up and down on my butt! Shontessa and Davon adjusted their turning so I was able to keep it up for a few bounces, then I rolled out of the rope. The crowd cheered. At least that's what they told me later—I was too much in a zone and didn't hear anything. All I could see was Davon watching me and turning to keep up with me and smiling a smile that said, *You go, girl!*

I didn't have much time to soak up the excitement because I had to take over the rope so Davon and Shontessa could jump. As I was turning, I snuck a glance over to Tameka and she caught my eye and gave me a thumbs-up. I felt warm all over, and it was a good warm feeling, not nervousness. I was thrilled that I had done something that made me feel electrified. I guess we *were* blazing! But then I turned my thoughts back to making sure I was turning the rope right because I heard Davon whisper, "Slow it down a bit!" and I felt the current of the rope change from Nia's end.

I slowed the rhythm, and then I saw Davon drop into the lunge jump we had seen the Jump Fuzions do. And a beat later, Shontessa was doing the lunge jump right along with him! Then they went back to doing the routine we had practiced, and then Davon jumped out to let Shontessa do her finale.

Shontessa did her pop ups, and they seemed especially high that night. Next, she did her hip-hop routine. Then she dropped down low in another lunge, and to close, she rolled out in a somersault, just like the Grant Elementary School team did. I heard a couple of "ooohhs" and "wows" from the audience. I was still feeling warm, but now it was a mixed-up feeling of being warm due to being proud of myself for my butt jumping and feeling hot and mad that Shontessa and Davon—especially Shontessa—had shown off, adding all that extra stuff while they were in the rope. But maybe their showboating would make us win.

Tameka hugged each of us, then all of us, in a clumsy, enthusiastic group hug. She went on and on about how fabulous we were and how we nearly scared her to death with all of our unplanned stunts. I was thinking about how my mistake turned into a showstopper. I thought about the African dancer. Did anyone realize my move had started off as a mistake? There was another break while the officials tabulated the scores. The announcer came to the microphone and said the three top teams were Grant Elementary School, Jump Fuzion, and Black Blaze but someone came up behind her and whispered something. The announcer came back to the mic and said they still needed to work something out with the scoring and would announce the winners in a few minutes and to please be patient.

I didn't say anything to my teammates or to Tameka, but I was thinking to myself, *Oh my God, oh my God, oh my God. I might actually win!* I would go home and tell Mom that I was going to be a Double Dutch superstar, just like she used to be. I would go to school tomorrow and be the most popular girl on Snapchat, Instagram, and *yo!*photo. I would replay this video online from now till now on. This would be the best night of my life.

One of the officials walked over to where me and the team were sitting. It was the lady from registration again. "Are you the adult in charge?" she said to Tameka.

"Yes, what is it?"

"Is Shontessa Adams one of your students?"

"Yes—well, she's not my student exactly." Tameka went on to explain she wasn't a teacher, just the grown-up who had chaperoned us. "But what's the problem?"

"This competition is for students age twelve and under. It's only for elementary school children," explained Ms. Registration. She thrust the registration form at Tameka. "Shontessa Adams attends Jefferson Middle School. Therefore, the team is disqualified."

"How can you say that? How can you do that?" I screamed. I felt my face crumple up and my hands cramped into tight fists. "She practiced with us. She worked hard just like everybody else—you can't do that!"

Tameka grabbed me and marched me out of the gymnasium. "Stop that, Jayla! I know you're disappointed, but you can't act like that!"

I jerked away from her and ran down the hallway. I sank to the floor and just sat there. Tameka started to come after me but must have thought better of it and just stood a ways away, watching me. After a few minutes, I heard the horn blare, meaning that the officials were ready to make their announcement. I didn't have to go back into the gym to hear them announce that second place was going to Jump Fuzion and first place was Grant Elementary School.

Our team got nothing. And the reason why? Shontessa. Or maybe I should blame Ms. McMillan. She scared away all the other kids at our school from being on the team. Or maybe it was just because it was April 1 and I was the biggest fool in the whole wide world.

CHAPTER 15

The Tuesday practice after the tournament was like going to a graveyard. Nobody showed up but Nia, and since you can't do much with just two people, I told her to go away. Ms. McMillan didn't even show up.

I finally cornered Ms. McMillan the following Wednesday.

"Where were you?" I didn't scream at her—both Mom and Tameka had told me I better not be disrespectful once I caught up with Ms. McMillan. But I knew I sounded plenty upset even though I kept my voice low.

"I had the day off. It was my birthday," she said, then smiled as if she was remembering how pleasant that day had been.

"Last Tuesday was the tournament."

"Oh, I completely forgot."

"How could you forget? It was our very first competition!" I could feel the tears welling up behind my eyes.

"Don't be upset. There will be another time. When God closes one door, He opens another one."

That's not even the way the expression goes. It's "When God closes one door, He opens a window." Either way it's not true, although grown-ups say that all the time. It was never going to be the same again. I didn't know if I'd ever get to do Double Dutch in front of an important crowd for an important prize.

It seemed like after the defeat, everybody figured that was the end of Double Dutch. Davon and Nia drifted off into other activities. Double Dutch became the unwanted pet shoved off to the animal shelter, something you used to love that you no longer had a place for. Because Double Dutch had died, it felt like a cloud was following me everywhere I went. Going to school wasn't as much fun now that there was no longer anything to look forward to once class let out.

One good thing was that now that spring was officially in town, we had plenty of pretty days outdoors. Some rainy days, too—it was April, after all—but we had some warm and sunny days. If our Double Dutch team were still meeting, I would've asked if we could take our practice out of the gym and onto the playground. During recess, I tried to get other kids to jump rope, but nobody was interested.

"Hey, Kierra and Jade. Wanna try Double Dutch? We have openings."

"We can't. We're on the cheerleading squad this spring," Kierra said as she and Jade strolled down the hall.

"Terrie, why don't you come back?"

"Is Ms. McMillan still in charge?" she asked. I didn't have to say anything—she knew the answer by reading the expression on my face. And I, in turn, knew Terrie's answer by reading the expression on *her* face.

"Hey, Kim. Basketball season is winding down. Want to try Double Dutch again?"

He looked at me as if I had a rash he didn't want to catch. He shook his head and walked away, dribbling his ball.

But I didn't tell Mom that the team had folded and so she kept practicing with me in the backyard. I was glad she jumped with me since the school team was dead and gone. We'd tie the rope to the fence and the other one of us would turn. Most days Shontessa joined us. I didn't know how to act around her. Seeing her reminded me of how awful everything had turned out. But when she was there, I had a better time jumping rope. It wasn't as good as having four or more people, but it was better than nothing.

What was surprising was to see Mom's spirits lift. She had as much fun jumping rope as me or Shontessa. And the positive energy seemed to carry over. Sometimes, she would turn on the radio and do a little dance while we fixed dinner or race me from the car to the door as if she were a kid like me.

April drizzled into May, and on the first Sunday of the month, Pastor Williams reminded everybody that Healthy Sunday would be happening in two weeks. Every year in May, my church held a health fair right after the Sunday service. Different clinics and people from various health organizations set up tables and would check your blood pressure, pass out flyers, and give away little gifts like pens, squeeze balls, and key chains. We'd been doing it for several years, and although it had started off small, now people from other churches would bring their people to our church's event.

"I don't have time to be healthy," my mother had said at last year's health fair and laughed. At the time, I didn't think it was anything serious because she made a joke about it. But now I felt a different kind of way.

While Pastor was telling the congregation about plans for the health fair, I noticed Antwon sitting one row ahead of me. He had a shiny oblong object in his hands—a new cell phone! Even Antwon had a phone and I still didn't. It wasn't fair. He was staring at the phone during the whole first part of church until Uncle Mike made him put it down.

"This year, in addition to the information booth, we're going to have some cooking demonstrations," Pastor said. I liked the sound of that. I wondered if the Krazy Krunchies company could come and give free samples. Mom had stopped buying them and I missed them. Although I liked making the salads for dinner, sometimes you need something crazy and crunchy to munch on.

Eating healthy food sometimes felt funny. Like when Mom told me we were going to Happy Hardware to buy food. Food from a hardware store? That didn't sound right. But she explained she was going to the nursery section where they sold plants. She bought some mint (which smelled wonderful!) and some basil (it had a springy, green scent) and some tomato seedlings.

Mom said we would use these plants in our cooking. The idea of that weirded me out. We made some iced tea, and Mom told me to break off some of the mint leaves to use. Pulling off leaves that had been growing in dirt didn't sound like something I wanted to put in my mouth. I felt more comfortable eating people-made food. She pointed out that when I make salad, I'm placing leaves on our plates to eat, so what was the difference? I didn't know, but breaking a leaf off a plant rather than taking lettuce out of a bag didn't seem natural.

Anyway, Pastor Williams was really hyped about the cooking part of the health fair. "We're going to show folks how to take soul food and make whole food—food that's good for body and soul."

If you want to make your body whole, I thought, *you need to do more than just feed it; you need to move it, too.* At the health fair, people would pick up the colorful brochures and take home a key chain as a souvenir, but they didn't really do anything. The people who were fat last year were still fat this year. Even watching a cooking demo and getting to taste a sliver of something really wouldn't make somebody feel something strongly enough to change. I began thinking that what would really be good for the health fair would be something to get people moving, to get them to actually take action.

Pastor Williams was winding up his remarks about the health fair. "Come to the health fair to learn the right thing to do. The whole human race got into trouble when Adam and Eve ate the wrong thing."

In front of me, I heard Antwon whisper to his daddy, "What was it that Adam and Eve ate?"

"An apple."

"I ate an apple yesterday for lunch!" said Antwon in distress. "Oh no! Am I in trouble?"

Poor Antwon. Having a new phone didn't make him any smarter.

After church, Antwon was showing off his phone to everybody. He was really excited about the new *yo!* photo app. It was just like Instagram but way more fly. All the teenagers were crazy about it. You could make pictures that told stories about what you were doing, and it was so easy to add special effects so that your life looked like a Hollywood movie. I moved away from where he was showing off his phone. The phone and the app hadn't made him smarter, but it did make him cooler around all the other kids.

Tameka and Alonzo were at church, too. Nowadays, they came all the time. They were standing on the steps outside chatting with other church members. Tameka was dressed up, and I had to admit she looked pretty. She wore a deep pink dress with green cuffs and a green collar, and she had on bright-green high heels. She looked like a spring blossom, a perfect outfit for a May day. And of course, her diamond ring was sparkling in the sunlight.

Cousin Alonzo caught sight of me and broke off his conversation to yell, "Hey, Jayla-Jayla! How's my favorite cousin?" He strode over to me and I gave him a high five. Tameka followed, trotting carefully on her four-inch heels.

"How's the Double Dutch team doing?" Alonzo asked.

"It's over," I mumbled.

"Maybe you can get it started again before school lets out." Tameka had caught up to me and Alonzo. "When I was in school, we kept going up until the very last day of school and then all through the summer. Especially the year we won the April First Double Dutch Jump-Off."

Yeah, yeah, rub it in, why don't you, I thought. But since I was at church, I tried to be nice.

"Nobody at school wants to be bothered. But I'm going to ask Pastor Williams if we can do a demonstration at the health fair."

"That's a great idea!" she said. Her enthusiasm was catching.

"That's a gorgeous dress."

"Why, thank you, Jayla," she said, giving me a surprised smile.

"Pink looks pretty on you," I added.

"Pink is one of the colors I picked for my wedding. We're set for the last Saturday in June."

June! That was only a month away! Alonzo was really going to marry this girl. I guess I could sorta see why he liked her. She was nice, and she was pretty, at least when she dressed up. And she was good at Double Dutch. Still, it made me sad that he was getting married. How could something be both good and bad at the same time?

———

Healthy Sunday arrived and church was full. "Don't forget the health fair in the fellowship hall!" called out Pastor Williams after the last amen.

But I *had* forgotten—I had meant to ask Pastor Williams if I could do a Double Dutch demonstration at the health fair. Now here was the day and I had dropped the ball.

Or the rope. Maybe if I had remembered, I could have recruited some kids to come out and play. I was as bad as Ms. McMillan. I had thought Double Dutch could become as popular as it was back in the day when my mother had done it. But I guess Double Dutch really was doomed.

Everyone streamed into the fellowship hall like a parade float gliding down an avenue. I went to a table with a red tablecloth and a big bowl of key chains shaped like fruits and veggies. As I took one that was a banana, the guy behind the table asked me, "Do you eat right, little lady?"

"I make the salad for dinner at my house," I told him.

"Great!" he said. "And do you exercise, too?"

"She's on the Double Dutch team at school." Tameka had followed me into the fellowship hall.

"What's Double Dutch?" the man asked.

"It's when you turn a rope going this way and then the second rope is going the other way and then—" I was making circles with my arms, but the puzzled look on his face told me he didn't get it.

He interrupted me to ask, "What? Is this some newfangled Nintendo thing that kids are doing?"

"No, it's not new. Even my mother used to do Double Dutch. You jump up and down using ropes going in different directions but side by side—"

I got interrupted again, but this time by Tameka. "We

can show you better than we can tell you." And then she whipped out a rope.

"You brought a rope?" I said, wondering what made her bring a jump rope to church.

"Remember earlier this month, you said you wanted to do a demo at the health fair? Remember I told you I thought it was a great idea?" Tameka thrust the ends of the rope in my hand, tugged on it, and started walking backward. We moved to the center of the room as we unrolled the rope. "Excuse me. Excuse me," I had to keep saying as I backward-bumped my way through. People stood back as we started turning the ropes, forming perfect arches. Over and under, *slap, slap*. Over and under, *slap, slap* in a beautiful rhythm. A person who is a good turner has a certain swing and flow in the way they turn. A good turner can make a bad jumper good. A good turner makes turning the rope feel like you're both dancing and daydreaming. You're concentrating real hard yet feeling free and easy at the same time. Tameka was a good turner. A very good turner.

But with both me and Tameka turning, neither one of us could jump. I was just about to say, "This isn't going to work," when from nowhere, a lady ran up and said, "Double Dutch! I love Double Dutch!" Then she jumped in. And she was fabulous. She was about as old as my mother, and she even did a few turnarounds in the rope before she missed.

"Ooh, that really took me back," she said. "I haven't jumped rope since the sixth grade!"

Next, a lady who looked familiar—but I couldn't quite place her—came up to us. She wore a bright yellow sundress that showed off her figure and high heels that showed off her legs. Her dress, her shoes, her purse, her jewelry—everything matched. She was skinny, but for some reason, she reminded me of elephants.

"Can I do it?" she asked.

"Sure!" I told her.

"Be our guest!" Tameka chimed in. We started turning again. But the woman just stood there and I realized she didn't know how to jump. We stopped the rope, and I had her stand midway between me and Tameka.

"When I shout, go, you're gonna hop just like this," I said while bouncing up and down with both feet together to demonstrate the bunny hop. She kicked off her heels and started jumping in her bare feet. Her toenails were painted a dazzling tropical orange and they matched her fingernails, like twenty tiny neon lights. We started turning the rope, but her step was off.

"Keep the rhythm," I said. "Let's try it again."

The next time, she started chanting. "Miss Mary Mack, Mack, Mack…" and when she got to the line, "She asked her mother for fifteen cents, to see the elephant jump over the fence," that's when I recognized her. She was the Miss Mary Mack lady we had met at church a few months ago.

"Look at that lady go!" shouted somebody on the sidelines.

And somebody else said, "That's her first time, but she got it now."

"I wanted to learn Double Dutch as a kid but never had the chance," said Miss Mary Mack as she put her shoes back on. "But now that I know how easy it is—and how much fun—I'm going to get everybody in on it!" Then she started rounding up people from all around the church.

Next thing I knew, a line had formed, and everybody who wasn't in line to jump was crowded around to cheer. My arms almost fell off from all the turning we had to do. Finally, Sister Arora took my end of the rope and said, "Chile, you wanna jump?" And of course I did.

I jumped in, and a few beats later, I felt a *whoosh* of air and heard footsteps behind me. Mom had jumped in, and soon she had matched her beat with mine and we were in perfect step.

"On the count of three, jump," whispered Mom. We did a C jump in unison. The audience hooted and cheered.

"Okay, how about a pop up?" I said. "One, two..." and on three, we not only did one pop up together, but we kept on doing them. We were like human popcorn kernels propelled into the air.

"Lawd Jesus, those two got it goin' on!" I recognized Deacon Tom praising us.

"Sister Sherry and her daughter got talent!" I don't know who said that because so many people were shouting and cheering.

The energy in the room had changed. It had gone from people having quiet, isolated conversations at the little tables scattered all around the room to every single eye riveted to the center of the fellowship hall, watching, grinning, and whooping. Their sparks gave me more peppiness and my peppiness fed their sparks.

We finished with Mom jumping in place while I moved around her so we ended up with our positions reversed. Then we both jumped out of the rope at the same time to wild applause and lots of hugs.

Antwon was running around, snapping pictures of us jumping to put on his *yo!*photo account. Deacon Johnson came up to me and said, "I'm the manager at the rec center. I need you to come and do what you just did for our kids."

Sister Ann grabbed my elbow and said, "I want you and your momma to do your thing at our family reunion this summer." And Mrs. Ebb, who worked for the local cable channel, said that Double Dutch was a perfect visual for a TV story and that she was going to tell the assignment editor about us—and by the way, did we have a card?

"Can I join your team?" a teen with long braids begged me at the same time that a grown-up asked my mother the same thing. Then two boys followed behind her asking to join, too. Wow. In just a few minutes, I had a whole crew of boys, girls, and grown-ups, plus a bunch of places to perform. Maybe I didn't need the school to have a Double Dutch team. Maybe Ms. McMillan was right for once. There *was* another opportunity.

CHAPTER 16

The next three weeks were the busiest days of my life. I'd been busier than the cafeteria when it's Fifty-Cent French-Fries Friday. After the health fair, we did a gazillion Double Dutch demos. Two days later, we did a store opening. Then the next Friday evening, we were at a wellness conference; on Saturday, an outdoor street festival; and a week later, another health fair.

There was a newspaper reporter at the health fair, plus Mrs. Ebb had told the producer at her job about us, and a reporter and a camera crew interviewed us on TV. Meanwhile, Antwon had made a *yo!* photo account for us in addition to Twitter and Instagram accounts, so everybody was following us. Even old people on Facebook had friended us because our team had grown-ups as well as young people on it. The grown-ups on the team were Mom, Tameka, and Miss Mary Mack, plus Cousin Julia. And it wasn't like Cousin Julia even *asked* to join—she *told* us she was going to be on the team. We also had two other family members and three teenagers who showed up from time to time, including Shontessa, who jumped with us regularly. Nearly all of them talked about how they had lost weight or gotten toned or just felt all around better as a result of the exercise they got from jumping rope. One cousin said Double Dutch gave her more energy and she was sleeping better. After the newspaper and TV stories hit, we really blew up. Mom's cell phone was beeping all the time with people requesting information or asking us to come to their event.

"This phone is driving me crazy," Mom said. "It never stops. It's like a tattoo on my ear drum."

"If you bought me a phone, I could help take calls," I said, but she ignored me. But even without juggling calls, I stayed just as busy as Mom. I had to go to school to rest 'cause, when at home, I was either rehearsing or performing or planning to rehearse or perform.

Sometimes we got paid for our exhibitions. Not that I ever saw the money. Cousin Julia put herself in charge of that, too. There were lots of people who would follow us from place to place, not because they wanted to be on the team, but just because they wanted to jump.

"I got a touch of sugar, baby. And my doctor told me I need to exercise in order to help bring my diabetes under control," said one of the church ladies who followed us.

"I want to be ready for swimsuit season," declared a twentysomething who often showed up at our demos. "And this is just the joint."

Cousin Julia put up a website for the group because so many people were trying to find out about us. The website also included health info, like how exercise helps make your heart strong. It can even make your brain smarter, improving your thinking and learning skills. How is it that something you do with your feet changes your brain? Double Dutch must have rebooted Cousin Julia's brain. She was the last person in the whole wide world I expected to launch a website. She's so old-fashioned and out-of-date when it comes to anything technological. I once heard her say, "Cell phones are a trick of the devil. They cause people to lose their ability to communicate."

How she came to that conclusion, I don't know. Cell phones do just the opposite—they help people talk all the time, everywhere. She then went on to say how young people didn't know how to talk to folks in person anymore because they were so glued to their phones, and some things didn't need to be posted online and life was better back before everything went digital...blah, blah, blah. So I was really surprised when she gave us a really sleek, eye-catching site. And I told her so.

"Technology is just like fire," she said. "It can cook your food up, or it can burn your house down. You just have to know how and when to use it."

The website had lots of videos of us in action. Plus, she had a bio under a picture of each team member, and she listed me as captain and founder! That really made Shontessa mad.

"I was there from the beginning, just like you." We were looking at the website on the computer at my house. Shontessa's mother had dropped her off because we were supposed to be having practice.

"But it was my idea to do it." I scrolled through the items on the website, so I didn't have to look at her.

"You didn't even know how to jump Double Dutch till I showed you." She made sure I saw her as she flung her hand in my face with her black fake fingernails flashing.

"It was my mother who taught me most everything I know how to do, not you. You're always too busy showing off to show anybody how to do anything."

"Are you two at it again?" Tameka had just arrived for rehearsal, and she walked over and stood between us.

Part of me was glad Tameka showed up to stop the arguing and part of me wanted to shut Shontessa up myself. I decided to leave it alone, and we went ahead and had our practice.

But the most exciting part—and the best payback to Shontessa—was when I saw the YouTube video of our Double Dutch demo at the farmers' market. They had been holding their kickoff for the season and had had us as part of the festivities. They had bins and baskets of cantaloupes so sweet you could smell them as you walked by and carrots with green ponytails and tomatoes in different colors, not just red but yellow and orange, and some were long and oval-shaped and others were round and beefy and a few were bumpy and ugly, but Mom said that often those tomatoes tasted the best.

It was the video for the farmers' market show that got ten thousand views on YouTube. There I was onscreen doing perfect pop ups, one after another. Shontessa's voice could be heard yelling, "I wanna go. When is it going to be my turn?" But I kept jumping for a long, long time before I missed, and she didn't even appear in that particular clip.

When the cable TV news crew came, they interviewed me and Mom. They interviewed Tameka. They interviewed Cousin Julia. Shontessa missed out on the interview because when she realized that we were going to be on television, she ran into the bathroom to put on some makeup. While she was doing that, she realized she had run out of her favorite lip gloss and ran down to the drugstore to buy some more. By time she did all of that, the news crew was packing up. But the interview with me and Mom was the one they used on the broadcast and that's the clip that went viral on the Internet.

The reporter liked the idea of a family jumping together. She was especially impressed by a mother and daughter jumping together. Her name was Sheridan Moy, and she had deep dimples and shoulder-length black hair that was cut so straight it looked like a tailor had hemmed it on a sewing machine. She wore a royal-blue dress with a square neckline that framed her face.

"Is it hard for people in the same family to work and play together?" she asked.

"Not for us," I told her, and I was glad Shontessa was nowhere around when I said it. I wondered if lying to a news reporter was a crime you could go to jail for.

"We're as crazy as any other family," Mom said, laughing. "But we know how to put the *fun* in *dysfunctional*."

"How old are you?" asked the reporter.

"She's eleven," Mom said, tilting her head toward me. "And when I jump into the rope, I'm eleven, too."

When Sheridan Moy asked Mom why she loved Double Dutch so much, I expected her to talk about how much she enjoyed it. But instead she told the reporter that Double Dutch had saved her life.

"I have high blood pressure. But once my daughter convinced me to jump Double Dutch, my pressure came down.

My doctor is pleased and I feel so much better. I also lost some weight, so I'm really happy about that!"

After our presentation at the farmers' market, we bought some fresh vegetables, but we still had to go to the grocery store to buy other stuff, like dish detergent and toilet paper. As we were heading out the grocery store, I stopped and took a look around. Nowadays, I always check out a store's parking lot. Is there an area with a lot of empty space? Can people at the entrance see the whole area? Is the pavement smooth enough for jumping? Ever since our start at the Happy Hardware lot and all the places where we've jumped since then, I automatically do a playground-CSI of any large open space. Once we got close to our car, we ran into Antwon and his dad, Uncle Mike.

"You've got quite a daughter!" said Uncle Mike. "I saw you jumping rope on TV."

"Yeah, I think I'll keep her," Mom said.

"You mean you can trade in your kids for better ones?" asked Antwon.

Me, Mom, and Antwon's daddy just looked at Antwon and shook our heads "Mike, I've got some good news to report," Mom said.

"More news? You seem to be on the news every night. What is it now—that you've bought stock in Krazy Krunchies and have made a million dollars?"

"No, I don't eat them like I used to. But that's not my good news."

"So what's the word?"

"One twenty-five over eighty."

"What's that? Your blood pressure?"

"Yes, it's gone down. Back at Christmastime, it was one fifty over ninety."

"Sherry, that's great! See what giving up Krazy Krunchies will do for you?"

"I don't think it was Krazy Krunchies. It was Jayla."

"Me? What did I do?" I asked.

"You got me jumping Double Dutch. I think the regular exercise did the trick."

"I can see you've shed some pounds. Maybe me and Antwon need to start jumping Double Dutch," Antwon's dad said, with a note of respect in his voice.

Antwon looked shocked at the idea.

"I could show you, Antwon," I said. "It's real easy. And lots of fun once you get started."

"But I'm not Dutch!" Antwon protested.

"C'mon, Antwon. Let me teach you right now," I said. "Mom, can you get the rope out the trunk?" Maybe Double Dutch could raise his IQ a few degrees.

"Right here?" Antwon and Uncle Mike asked simul-taneously.

"Parking lot jump rope is our specialty," said Mom as she ran to the car.

"You can jump, too," I told Uncle Mike.

"Well, actually, at the church health fair, I was told my pressure was a touch high. Maybe Double Dutch is something I should consider," he said thoughtfully.

"Okay, Antwon, jump like this. C'mon and do it with me," I said as I did a bunny hop. And Antwon did it, right in step with me.

When Mom came back, she and I started the rope, that rhythmic *slap, slap, slap*, making that beat that always makes me want to jump in and make my own feet join the rhythm. I once heard an athlete interviewed who said when he was playing really well, he stopped being a man manipulating a ball. He said he and the ball became all one thing, a compelling, continuous flow of energy. Turning makes me feel kind of the same way. In a dreamy zone, yet more aware all at the same time.

"Hey, Jayla! I want a go!"

Who was that calling me and breaking my concentration? I turned to look.

"Davon!"

He was wearing his black T-shirt and black pants and black high-tops, just as if he were set to do a tournament. And boy, did he do a show. Davon ran over and immediately dived into the rope, swooping past Antwon like a jet plane.

"Wow! Look at him!" Antwon gushed.

Davon did a Running Man move, spun around, did a pop up, then a few jumps where he kicked his legs out in front, then in back of him. Then he just did some hard, intense jumping. Antwon must've been studying Davon hard because, when Davon jumped out, he jumped in and was stomping like he had always known how to jump. When he missed, I was expecting him to ask me what to do to keep jumping longer. But what he said was, "Show me how to work the ropes."

So I gave him my end and explained how to make arcs with his arms as he turned. Without me having to tell him, he saw that the way he turned the rope could help a jumper jump. He automatically seemed to know when to go fast or when to slow down. He changed the rhythm to help the jumper flow. And he was strong. He could keep turning on and on and on, which was really good when Davon was in the rope because Davon could last a long time. Antwon kept up the pace, and when Davon finally jumped out, he gave Antwon a hearty high five.

"Man, you know the ropes," Davon told Antwon. "How long you been doing this?"

"About fifteen minutes," Antwon said.

"No, no, I mean, how long have you been doing Double Dutch?"

"Today is my first day."

"Man, you know what you doing."

I couldn't believe it. Finally, something Antwon was smart at.

When we finally got in the car and were alone together, there was something I had to ask.

"Mom, did Double Dutch really help make you healthy?"

"It did, Jayla. I knew I needed to exercise, but I kept putting it off. You motivated me to get back into Double Dutch— something I love almost as much as you." She hugged me. "And something I needed to do to get fit. If you hadn't persisted and kept nagging me to do it"—and she gave me a funny grin to let me know she wasn't fussing at me—"I'd be so much worse off. You got me to get a jump on being strong and healthy. And in such a fantastic way! Who knew working out doesn't have to be work? It can be fun."

"I wish more people knew that."

"Thanks to you, now they do."

"So, do you think I'm…" I wanted to say *smart*, but that sounded like bragging.

"I think you're a leader," Mom said. "You get a good idea and put it into action. And people are happy to go along with you."

"I think I like being a leader."

"You're a good one."

I felt real proud that something I had done had helped so much. Even with all the trouble with Ms. McMillan and Shontessa and the terrible way the tournament turned out, if it made my mother get better, it was worth it. I thought we were headed home, but once in the car, she turned in the opposite direction from our house.

"Where are we going now?"

"You and I are going shopping."

"Back to Happy Hardware?"

"No, to the mall."

"What for?"

"You need a new dress for Alonzo's wedding."

Oh. Alonzo and Tameka's wedding was next Saturday. Alonzo, my favorite cousin, was really going to marry Tameka. When I really thought about it, I supposed Tameka wasn't so bad. She had turned out to be a better grown-up than Ms. McMillan. And she'd probably be a nicer relative than Shontessa. And Alonzo liked her. I guessed I liked her, too.

I almost never wear dresses. I wear pants to school every day, and then I come home and change into jeans. I wear skirts to church, but I only have one on for the morning service and then it's right back to pants once I get back to the house. But if I had to wear a dress for the wedding, I wanted a pretty dress. Tameka wasn't the fanciest female I knew, but when she dressed up for church, she was in fashion. She wore bright colors, but without too much frilly stuff going on—just the right mix of girly and cool. I wanted to get the same effect. I wanted everybody to look at me and think, *She looks good,* not *Aww…how cute.*

We looked at thousands of dresses and I got tired. I could feel myself turning cranky. Then we saw it. Mom and I knew at the same time *that* dress was the one. It was pretty but something I could be comfortable in. It was a deep peachy color with sleeves that came to my elbow and a scoop neck with a deeper, luscious pink ribbon threaded around the neckline. The dress flared out just a little around my knees. The same ribbon went around the hem. When I tried it on and did a turn to make the hem swirl out, Mom smiled and smiled even though it looked like she was wiping a tear away. "My little girl," she kept saying. But I thought I looked rather grown up. When I took a look at myself in the mirror, I felt like I was wearing the perfect dress.

I wonder if that's the way Cousin Alonzo had felt when he met Tameka, that after trying out a lot of pretty ones, here was the one that was a good fit.

Maybe Tameka felt the same way about him.

I realized I felt the same way about them both.

CHAPTER 17

There are so many things to love about June. School ends and summer starts. Swimming pools and barbecues. Camp-outs and cookouts. And weddings.

We were at a rec center, gearing up to do a demonstration. This event was the opening session for a series of demos we were contracted to do at all the recreation centers in the city. This center was huge, with a basketball court, a meeting room, and I could smell a hint of chlorine from the Olympic-size indoor pool. Mom was off to the side of the playground where she was speed jumping with a single rope. I was doing stretches. Shontessa was stretching, too, but every few minutes, she pulled out her mirror to make sure her hair wasn't out of place. As we did our warm-up, Tameka told us that she and Alonzo were going to jump the broom at their wedding.

"Why you want to do that?" asked Shontessa, scrunching up her face. "Isn't that something slaves used to do?"

"It's a sweet tradition. A lot of couples do it to honor our ancestors," Tameka explained.

"So what do you do exactly?" I asked. I pictured Tameka holding a mop like it was a dance partner and skipping around with it.

"The broom is laid down on the floor, and we hold hands and together we 'jump into the land of matrimony,'" she said, smiling at the thought of it.

I wasn't sure if that sounded like a good idea or not. But I didn't think more about it because a man with a bullhorn was calling for us to get started.

As always, we had so many people waiting to jump, the line could have reached all the way to Mars. But each of us took turns turning and coaching and jumping, and we managed to whittle the line down to an earth-to-moon length. We didn't care because we were having fun. And once we got into that Double Dutch zone, time disappeared. At least for me.

I had noticed an older lady, kind of stout, who watched us from the side of the area. She wore a dusty brown wig and a beige tracksuit. She was the type who could blend into the background except she was so ultra-ordinary that she stood out among all the laughing, chatting, playing people in the room. I could feel her eyes on us even when I wasn't looking in her direction. As time passed, she inched closer and closer and got in line. When it was finally her turn, she got in the rope on a shaky start but literally found her feet. Me and Shontessa were turning for her, and eventually we all hit the right rhythm. She was all energy: smiling, jumping, more smiling, bouncing, a couple of crisscrosses, then she shut down. She didn't miss. She. Stopped. Dead.

"Oh no, did I hit you with the rope?" I ran over to her. So did Shontessa. The woman's shoulders trembled and she sniffled; her head was down. When she looked up, tears were standing in her eyes.

"Thank you," she said softly. "It's just that I haven't felt that much joy in a long while."

I didn't know what to say. But Shontessa made the right move. She hugged her.

"We love doing this," Shontessa said. "Come back anytime and get as much joy as you can stand."

The lady hugged each of us and left. Before we could say anything to each other, a kid was yelling, "C'mon, it's my go!"

"My knees are telling me it's time to go," said Cousin Julia, who was working a second rope with my mother. "We were hired to do two hours. It's going on two and a half. Let's roll out."

"But look at all these people," I said. Shontessa nodded in agreement. "We should stay a little longer for them."

Cousin Julia walked up to the line. "Here's our card. Check out the schedule on our website," she said. "And meet us at the next gig." She and Mom passed out business cards as they made their way to the door. But the people who hadn't had a chance to jump yet turned their faces to us like hungry orphans.

"I'm willing to stay longer," Shontessa said.

"I'll stay longer, too," Tameka said.

"Who's going to stay with you? Shontessa and Jayla are riding with me," Mom said.

"I'll see that they get home," Tameka said and then turned to face me. "Let's get these people in the rope."

We kept turning. It was such a great time watching each person. There was a first-grade girl who keep circling back in line to get one more turn. We invited a grown man to try it and he said, "Absolutely not!" but then he saw another man do it, and he decided to jump—and was good at it! We got everybody in the rope from kindergartners to college kids to Social Security seniors. People's feet were laughing, their hearts were dancing, and if their muscles were aching, it was in a good way.

I got a surprise when a lady and her daughter walked in. When I saw them, Cousin Julia's frowning face popped in my mind, the face she makes whenever she talks about cell phones. Oh! It was the mother and daughter who had visited our church the Sunday after Thanksgiving—and who gotten the phone call in the middle of the service. When they came in, I ran over to the little girl to say hello.

"I remember you!" I said. "Maya, right?" I looked at the girl, who smiled at me. "And you're Ms. Miner?"

"You've got a great memory," Ms. Miner said. "We noticed all the activity going on and decided to see what was happening."

"You wanna jump?" I asked, looking back and forth between both of them, waiting to see who wanted to go first.

"I don't know how," Maya said shyly.

"But your enthusiasm is making me want to try!" said Ms. Miner.

"None of these people knew how until now!" And we proceeded to show Ms. Miner and Maya what to do. After a while, I took a short break and me and Maya sat off to the side.

"How long will you be in town?" I asked her.

"We've just moved here. My mother's job transferred her to DC."

I told her that we should definitely keep in touch.

"I was afraid it was going to be hard to make friends, but now that I've run into you, I feel like already have one!" Maya said. She gave me a quick hug.

It was funny how that happened. I lost one Maya because her father's job took her away from DC. But now I'd found a new Maya to be a friend because her mother's job brought her to DC.

"Why are you sitting down talking while I'm standing up turning?" Shontessa called over to me. So I got up and took Shontessa's end. She immediately cut in front of the next person in line and took an impromptu turn, repeating some of her tournament moves. I was going to fuss at her for busting in the line, but none of the people waiting got mad at her. The crowd whooped and broke out into applause. So I didn't get mad, either, and just yelled, "Go, Shontessa!" along with everyone else.

It was in the middle of all these cheers and shouts and smiles that Alonzo marched into the gym and made a beeline for Tameka.

"What are you doing still in here? I've been waiting in the car for you for nearly thirty minutes!"

"Oh." Tameka looked truly surprised.

"Your text said five more minutes twenty minutes ago."

"We've got a lot of people who want to jump." Tameka gestured at the people still waiting to get a turn.

"What about me? If you wanted to spend all day and all night doing Double Dutch, you should have driven instead of asking me to pick you up."

"You want to jump, Cousin Alonzo?" I asked. Maybe he was mad because we hadn't included him.

"I don't think so."

"Oh, come on," Shontessa said. "Or do you think you can't do it?"

Alonzo ignored Shontessa and spoke to Tameka. "Let's go so I can take you home."

"We have to drop off Shontessa and Jayla first."

"What?"

"Sherry and the others already left. I'm sorry. I didn't think. I was so caught up in the excitement."

He looked from Tameka to Shontessa to me and back again.

"It's mostly my fault, Cousin Alonzo," I said to him. "Don't be mad at Tameka."

All he said was, "Anybody who's riding with me needs to leave now."

He turned and headed for the exit. Me and Shontessa hurriedly rolled up the rope.

"All right, we're coming," Tameka said, then turned to the waiting jumpers. "I guess that's it for today. But follow us online to see where we'll be next!" She shrugged and held up her hands at the line of people who weren't going to get a go, and we all scurried to catch up with Alonzo as he strode out the door.

In the car, nobody was saying nothing; it felt like Alonzo was still a little bit mad with us. If only he had taken a moment to join in with Double Dutch, that would have put him in a good mood.

"Cousin Alonzo, you're just about the only person in the family who hasn't jumped," I told him.

"Somebody has to keep both feet on the ground."

"You'd like it if you tried it," Shontessa said.

"My toes voted against it ten to one," Alonzo said.

"It wouldn't hurt if you got more exercise," Tameka chided him.

"Does *running late* count as exercise?" Alonzo said with a slight attitude. "If so, I got plenty of exercise today."

"You act like I meant to mess things up," Tameka said back to him. "Take a chill pill."

"You all don't sound like people who are getting married in a few weeks," Shontessa said. I was in the back seat, so I couldn't see their faces, but I could feel the heat from Tameka and Alonzo throbbing through the air. Not that that bothered Shontessa.

"When I get married, I'm not going to let my husband disagree with me. He's going to do everything I tell him to do, so we won't ever fight."

"*Shut up, Shontessa!*" Me, Tameka, and Alonzo all said it at the same time and that broke the tension and changed the atmosphere in the car.

Then I started chanting: "Alonzo and Tameka, sitting in a tree…"

Shontessa joined me on the next line: "K-I-S-S-I-N-G. First comes love, then comes marriage, then comes Tameka with the baby carriage."

After we sang the chant all the way through, me and Shontessa sang it again. This time, Alonzo and Tameka joined in at the K-I-S-S-I-N-G part, and we all laughed and sang together. The chanting rearranged the mood.

It reminded me of church, everybody singing, even people whose voices—or choices—were not perfect. It worked, not because we sounded good but because we all joined in together.

———

Alonzo and Tameka's wedding was scheduled for the last Saturday in June at 11:00 a.m. We showed up at church early so we could get good seats.

"Are you here for the bride or groom?" asked the usher as we entered.

"Both!" I piped up.

The knot of people close by all laughed.

"We're family of the groom," Daddy said, and he and Mom led the way down the aisle. I stepped up right behind them when one of the ushers appeared at my side. The usher took me by the arm and escorted me to my seat. It made me feel important, like I was a rapper's girlfriend with a backstage pass. The church was pretty much full, and Alonzo was standing at the front looking as handsome as a king, a rock star, and a superhero all rolled into one.

The service began, and Tameka and her dad came down the aisle together. Her wedding dress wasn't a poufy gown. Although it had layers of fabric that made it stand out, it came in tight at the waist, flared out, and stopped just below her knees. She wore a veil that draped over long, elegant braids. I've never met a princess, but if I did, I'm sure she would look like that.

Everybody was looking at her. Was she nervous? I knew I would be. She didn't look nervous. Maybe all the Double Dutch shows we had done had been good practice for this. But I think I'd still be jumpy inside if all that attention was zeroing in on me.

Pretty soon the most important moment of the ceremony happened.

"I now pronounce you husband and wife," boomed Pastor Williams. I knew the next thing that would happen would be the kissing part. The idea of it made me giggle and my eyes were stuck on Alonzo to watch him do it.

But when Pastor Williams declared, "You may now kiss the bride!" Alonzo said, "Wait a minute." Everybody froze and stared. Alonzo pulled out his phone and turned to the congregation.

"I have to update my Facebook status from single to married."

Everybody laughed—I could hear Cousin Julia groan all the way in the back. Next, Tameka whipped out her phone and said, "Let me be the first to like your new status!"

Then Alonzo gave Tameka the biggest hug and kiss I'd ever seen in my life, and the whole entire church broke out with applause. I might've clapped the loudest and grinned the widest. Tameka and Alonzo were grinning pretty big, too. I could feel their happiness radiating out from them like rays of sunshine spreading over everyone in the room.

The reception was held in the fellowship hall where they'd had the health fair last month. But it was decorated so pretty it looked totally different. There were flowers on every table and streamers wrapped around the poles in pink and white and a ten-story-tall cake with a tiny bride and groom on top of it.

Antwon was running around snapping pictures with his cell phone, standing right beside the official picture taker who had a real camera. At first it was fun to sit and watch everyone greet each other and check out what all the ladies were wearing. But after a while, it got kind of boring. There's not much to do at a wedding besides repeat the same chitchat with family members. This was almost as bad as Thanksgiving except instead of being at home in comfortable clothes, you were at church in fancy clothes. I saw cousins I hadn't seen since Christmas. Tommy and Kwame were there, of course. I hoped they wouldn't mess things up—although as it got boringer and boringer, I was kinda hoping they'd do a little something exciting.

We were sitting around waiting for our table to get called up to the buffet line. I was seated with a bunch of other kids. Shontessa was seated with the teenagers, which made me a little jealous because she didn't get put with the little kids. But I was also glad I didn't have to sit around her.

It seemed like they deliberately called every table ahead of the kids' table. It wasn't fair that the kids had to go last. Alonzo and Tameka got to go first. I guess that made sense, since it was their party, but still, I hated having to wait.

Once I got my plate, the food wasn't all that great. The things they served were dainty and colorful, not something to fill your belly. It reminded me more of origami than a real meal. I ate a teeny tiny sandwich with something green in between, then I filled up on punch. Antwon separated the slices of bread and took a picture of whatever was in the middle. I decided to save space for the cake.

But after everybody had eaten, they didn't cut the cake. The DJ started playing music. "And now we'll have the first dance of Mr. and Mrs. Alonzo Reed!" announced the DJ.

Alonzo led Tameka out onto the floor. Once in the

middle of the room, Alonzo held up his hand to catch everyone's attention and to make people stop talking. When everybody settled down, he said. "Normally, when a couple gets married, their first official act is to dance together. But we're going to do things a little bit differently."

Oh, I said to myself, *now is when they're going to jump the broom.* I saw my mother come out with a large tote bag and place it at their feet.

"My wife"—Alonzo paused after saying the word *wife* as if it were an especially sweet piece of candy and he wanted to enjoy every drop of it—"is someone who likes to stay one jump ahead."

He reached into the bag and pulled out a miniature broom decorated with kente cloth and set it down before them. I remembered seeing African dancers wearing colorful kente cloth when they performed. Tameka had told me that a long time ago, only royalty would wear kente. "Our first act of matrimony is to jump the broom."

He grabbed her hand, she used her other hand to hold on to her dress, and they both hopped over the broom together.

"Awww" came from some in the crowd. Others clapped and smiled.

"And now we're going to jump again. But this time, I'm one jump ahead of her." And he reached into the bag and pulled out two sets of jump ropes. One set of Double Dutch ropes and one short rope like the kind a boxer uses to train with. I noticed Mom walking out onto the dance floor. What was going on?

"My wife loves to jump Double Dutch. And she thinks I can't jump. But I'm here to show her I'm one step ahead of her." Tameka looked puzzled, especially when Alonzo handed one end of the rope to her and one to my mother. Tameka started to smile as she began turning.

Alonzo had his short rope in hand, draped around the back of his knees. He jumped in the Double Dutch rope, and then, once he had his pace going, he started jumping using the single rope at the same time as he was jumping Double Dutch! To do that, he had to obey two different rhythms at the same time. Everyone in the audience hooted and hollered and cheered. Who knew he even knew how to jump up and down, much less do a complicated move like that? I screamed Alonzo's name over and over, I was so excited. I knew that would be my next new stunt. I couldn't wait to figure it out so I could do it.

When Alonzo missed, Tameka ran over to him and kissed him and hugged him and laughed and made over him.

"Where did you learn how to do that?" I heard her say.

"A man has his secrets" is all he said. But from the expression I saw on Mom's face, I think she taught him that trick. And now she'd better teach me, too.

Alonzo eased over to me and whispered, "Jayla-Jayla, I'm going to do the same thing at your wedding."

Antwon ran up and picked up the end of the rope that Tameka had dropped when she ran over to embrace Alonzo.

"Who else wants a turn?" he yelled.

And before you knew it, there was a long line of friends and family waiting to jump. I was first in line. Now I was glad I hadn't eaten much or I wouldn't have been able to jump as hard and long as I did. I never knew when they cut the cake because I spent all of the remainder of the time jumping and turning.

You'd think people would find it a bit weird to jump rope at a wedding reception. But everybody had something good to say about Double Dutch:

"This is something I could do every day."

"Can you bring this to my school?"

"Workin' out ain't my thing, but I sure do like to play."

Almost as much fun as jumping was watching everybody else jump. Cousin Julia kicked off her high heels and started jumping in her stocking feet, but because her pantyhose made her feet slip, she ended up falling on her butt and everybody laughed. At first, I thought she was going to be mad, but she ended up laughing, too.

I was wondering why Kwame and Tommy hadn't gotten up to trouble; with all the motion and commotion,

I would have thought they'd be right in the middle of it all. The only one of them I saw was Kwame, and he was quieter than usual. Later, when Alonzo was looking for his single rope, we found Kwame had used it to tie up Tommy in the basement.

My favorite part of the wedding happened after the wedding. Or rather, it happened at the wedding but I didn't know it until the wedding was all over. Antwon took pictures of me at the wedding. He got one of me and Tameka jumping in midair while holding hands. Alonzo and Shontessa were both in the shot too, turning. I was high in the rope, grinning big. The hem of my dress ballooned out. It looked like I was floating and my skirt was my parachute.

That was one fabulous shot. It was a great moment when he took the picture and it was a great moment when I saw the picture later. It showed off everything I was feeling about everything. I was thrilled that Alonzo had thought to bring my favorite thing—Double Dutch—to be a part of his wedding. And the fact that he knew it was a favorite thing for me and Tameka made it doubly delightful. And to see Antwon do something he was actually good at, that was a double delight, too—he was skillful at turning the rope *and* he was good at catching the best moment in the rope. That day was not only just a happy day for Double Dutch, it was a doubly happy day in every way.

The weekend after the wedding, we were at Cousin Julia's house for a Double Dutch rehearsal when Shontessa showed me the picture. We had taken a break and had come indoors to flop on her cushiony green chairs and soak up some air conditioning. But that photo wasn't the only one. Antwon had taken lots of them. He had several good pictures of Shontessa, too. The best photo was one of her speed jumping with her braids flying like skinny flags from the back of her head. Even though it was a still picture, you could feel the speed racing off her limbs and passing you by with a breeze.

"That's the one I posted on Instagram," she said, and then shook her head so her braids swung from side to side, all in my face. "Which one are *you* posting on your Instagram account?"

"I don't have one," I said, which she already knew. She just wanted to rub in the fact that I was phoneless.

"Oh yeah," she said. "I guess little kids can't be on social media."

"You kids spend way too much time on social media," Cousin Julia said.

Oh no. Here we go, I thought. Cousin Julia was going to start lecturing us again about the evils of technology. She had made prints of the pics and was carefully inserting our photos in the same book that held her grandbabies' photos.

"Stop screwing up your face, Jayla," she said. "You're one

197

of the few young people I know who doesn't always have her face stuck to a screen. You *do* things. You have a real life, not just a virtual life."

"Well, I wouldn't mind if I had a screen of my own to look at now and then," I said.

"*Now and then* is the operative concept," declared Cousin Julia. "Technology should be one ingredient, not the whole meal. It's the salt and pepper, not the meat and potatoes."

"Can you actually eat technology, Cousin Julia?" asked Antwon, putting a corner of his phone in his mouth. "Is that why they call it an Apple?"

After we all fell out laughing, Cousin Julia turned back to me. "I was talking to Sherry about you." *Oh no*, I thought again. Although I wasn't going to get the "dangers of digital" lecture, evidently I was in trouble for something else. Had Antwon done some stupid thing that was being blamed on me?

"You know, we've made a bit of money from our Double Dutch demos," she continued.

"And I've been putting your share away toward your college fund," Mom said.

"I know," I said. "But it would be nice if I could spend some now."

"I agree. There's a little room in the budget for extras. Julia is the one who helped me to see that."

I turned to look at Cousin Julia with a question mark on my face.

"Since it was you who started the Double Dutch phenomenon, I think you should be the first one to profit from your smart idea," Cousin Julia said. I didn't know where she was going with that.

And then she held out a box.

It was a smartphone! It was sleek and shiny, with a glossy, big screen (bigger than Shontessa's), and I couldn't wait to start adding apps to make it the smartest smartphone ever. Shontessa was looking at me with the same expression she'd worn when she realized that the video that featured me—not her—went viral.

"Thank you a million, zillion times! Thank you!" I screamed.

"You earned it," said Cousin Julia.

"You deserve it," Mom said, beaming. But not beaming as much as me. I was doubly, doubly happy. I started jumping up and down because I couldn't hold in all the happiness that was bouncing around inside of me.

"If you're going to do all that jumping around, we might as well start up the rope again," said Cousin Julia.

And that's exactly what we did.

ACKNOWLEDGMENTS

Writing is an alone-in-a-quiet-space activity while Double Dutch is a gang-of-folks-in-a-loud-place activity. So writing a book about Double Dutch is a combination of both. I have a lot of people who cheered me on in this project.

I didn't think I had anything new to say about Double Dutch until Sara Camilli planted the idea.

DC Retro Jumpers—I love y'all! Thanks to the original regulars: Leslie Bournes, Debbie Gibbs, Mr. Jimmie, Lorraine Jones-Wardlaw, Monica Marcelli, Myra Morgan Martin, Josephine Morris-Young, Carlyle Prince, Gloria Ray and her husband, Bettie Robinson-Gibbs, Camille Sabbakhan, Tamika Washington Shingler, and Robbin Ebb who elevated DC Retro Jumpers to a whole other level.

Shout-outs to Shirley Debrow, who first opened The Rec to us; Mary McBride, who literally took DCRJ around the world; Christina Pulles, editor extraordinaire; and Jackie Grice, who knows all my secrets.

Major love to the Friday arts group who listened to all my struggles, especially Shelley, Dot, Magda, Martie, Mary, Rob, and Doris; and to the Wednesday Night Writers who read the book in its first draft: Tom Adams, Shabnam Afora Afsah, Elizabeth Bruce, Cheryl Miner, Michael Oliver, Anne Pellicato, and chief cheerleader Phil Kurata. The book would not have been completed without you.

Thanks to SCBWI, and the crew at Francis Gregory Neighborhood Library. Vita Washington—I'm still waiting for you to get in the rope.

And thanks most of all to my mother, Marilyn F. Jones, who not only taught me how to read but instilled in me the joy of reading.